MITCH ROBINSON

THE PAST ALWAYS CATCHES UP. IT IS JUST A MATTER OF WHEN.

THE CROOKED CHAIN OF GHOSTS

PART I

22:10 Part I: The Crooked Chain of Ghosts

Copyright 2015 © Thomas Mitchell Robinson
ISBN: 978-0-9861026-0-8

First edition.
Library of Congress Cataloging-in-Publication Data is on file
with the Library of Congress

PART I

THE CROOKED CHAIN OF GHOSTS

CHAPTER 1

Once more the knife crossed to join the fork. Last bits of carrot and gravy were pushed and lifted, leaving the modest white plate nearly clean, although a narrow, faintly brown smear remained across the plain surface. Nevertheless, a satisfied Nikolai Sergiyevich Tarasov lowered the cutlery in finish and glanced at the clock hanging on the wall.

It was 22:10. He would be late.

Unlike most people, this realization did not trigger a need to hurry in Nikolai. It was not his nature; an easy serenity pervaded his entire being. Rushed time was merely a bird's shadow passing over a crisp mountain lake—in the transience, stillness remained. His father had noticed the trait in the toddler early and often remarked ever after that it was a gift from his mother's side of his family.

Maybe it was the quality that helped Nikolai endure nights like this one the most. Any normal person would have been a wreck by now under the strain of such duplicity. Somewhere deep down, he intuitively knew this was so, but he was not one to question his own feelings in the moment. Self-absorption was not his nature either; Nikolai tended to be more interested in the events and people around him. He could sit in silence for long periods of time, just gazing at the intersecting contours of reality toying with each other in his mind. A look of distant bemusement would evidence itself and freeze across his face. Sometimes, he had to be snapped out of the trance. This was one of those times.

Nikolai took a deep breath and leaned back in his chair after completing the meal. Before him stood a woman, facing away and leaning over a sink. He was especially struck by the mingling of her straight and curved lines. Her dark hair was pulled back taut into a twisted ball, revealing the smooth slope of her neck in the dull, malted luminescence of the outdated pendant light over the table. In a rapid succession, she reached to her side and took in her hands from the kitchen counter a cup, a plate, a few forks, spoons, and knives. One by one, they disappeared in front of her followed by the rolled tensing of her upper body, the sound of water interrupted in its fall, and clanks against a cheap stainless steel basin.

Nikolai's eyes drifted lower to her shoulders, which were snuggly covered by a black polyester-cotton, long-sleeve top. The smooth symmetry was abruptly broken by a black belt and then naturally perfected lower again by a firm muscular arc and the long trim vertical descent of her dark-gray, slim, wool trousers. Everything about her whispered a sleek, minimalist aesthetic. Everything—except the socks. Frayed, lime-colored cotton socks screeched out from between the dark trousers and the well-worn tile floor.

These bursts of green shifted and stretched in the slowed distortion of his daydream, and, at this moment, the socks commanded his gaze. They were not new; in fact, they had been with her for longer than he had known her. Nearly identical pairs Nikolai had bought for her had vanished to the bottom of her drawer, never to be used. This particular pair, mended so many times as to be arguably a wholly evolved new creation that replaced the original, were an enduring bit of comfort she reached for after work or on the weekends.

In that way, they had become something of a life constant, but, from time to time, Nikolai would see them revealed in an original way, as he did now. Her lime-green socks were, like other things that could dispatch Nikolai's imagination and gaze, small treasures of the absurd juxtaposed against an otherwise mundanely solemn moment. He collected such beautiful misfit images and tinkered with them in his mind.

Now the rambling socks slowed, paused, and then spun around as she turned off the water and wiped her hands on a towel. In his peripheral vision, Nikolai could see the woman run her fingers back over her hair and puff out her cheeks as she exhaled in exhaustion. She looked down at her husband, and he felt her notice the distant stare in his eyes.

"Where have you gone now, Kolya?" she asked playfully and tenderly as she approached him. Moving the back of her still slightly damp hand down his cheek, she held his chin between her thumb and index finger. At the sound of his diminutive name, Nikolai's thoughts gently returned to the present, and he met her warm gaze with his own soft-brown eyes.

He reached up and guided her around the small table to sit across his lap. For a man who spent so many hours at a desk, Nikolai was stocky and chiseled, so shifting her tall womanly figure required little effort. He wrapped his arms around her waist, and she adored the security of his strong embrace. Nikolai admired the base of her neck and the barely exposed

4

view of her chest from the low cut of her top. Each and every part of her was profoundly sensual. He knew every inch one thousand times over, yet arousal ceaselessly found him anew whenever elements of her body were inadvertently revealed—as though being seduced again for the first time through small, measured glimpses of her nakedness.

"I'm here," he replied.

"Is that so? Are you really here, darling? You've been fading off into your own world more often lately. What's going on?"

"Thank you for dinner," he said, looking up at her. "I love you for so many reasons, not least of which is your mother's *podzharka* recipe." He smiled and kissed her lips softly. It was a genuine, if feeble, attempt to change the subject.

She paused and took a deep breath. Nikolai sensed that her silent response was to let his words simply settle uncomfortably in the room.

She rested one hand against his chiseled face, feeling the late-day stubble beneath her palm, while the other ran back and forth slowly through his hair. Some Russian women would have quickly burned white-hot when their men so obviously avoided an emotional question. Instinctively, these women might have produced a tantrum in an effort to provoke their lovers into revealing more. She did not. In part, because she knew a flash tempest would have little effect on him—he was caring and secure, and he was too good of a man in that way.

And also in part because there was something different, too, about her. She did not want to fall into the trap of becoming a woman who, like Pavlov, habituated her husband into demands and offerings, a relationship that over the years would cannibalize both itself and her as the triggers became ever larger and impossible to satisfy. For her, the journey of love was gradual and restrained—more than mere pragmatism, less than mere passion. This was the lesson she had learned from watching her own mother anyway. But in retrospect, she remained calm because something was in the air tonight: a feeling, a silent voice that both calmed her and counseled her to let things be. Instead, she watched him carefully, lovingly.

And then she saw it.

It was the first time in all the years she had known Nikolai that she actually watched it happen. Possibly, it was the first time in memory that it had even happened at all. As she leaned in for another kiss, the silence and closeness unsettled him and he twitched, a nervous shudder in which the emotional pressure built up in his core reflexively collapsed and let go. The surface effect was slight but noticeable; he awkwardly disengaged and glanced at the clock again. And then he caught himself and tried to cover it.

Now she knew something was wrong. But why the clock? It was after 10:00 p.m. Why check the time? Then she realized why, and it set off a cold feeling inside her.

He, likewise, knew she had noticed. Nikolai was quietly furious with himself for the slip. He wrapped his arms around her and pulled her closer.

"When do you have to go?" she asked flatly.

"I'm late already."

"But Kolya..."

"I'm sorry."

"Tonight was supposed to be free."

"I'm sorry."

"You're not here *again*."

He pushed back a little so he could see her clearly. "What are you saying?"

She sighed. "This is what I mean. You're never here anymore. With me. With us." She waved to the door of the kitchen leading into the living room. "You're either at work, or when you are here, you drift off into your daydreams."

"But that is me. That is the man you married," he said calmly.

"No, it's not...no, *it is not*. This is new. Before, you were always home at night. You have always had time for me and Stasya. There was work, yes. I know you enjoy the business life, the challenge, the pace...the success. But there was a lock on the door of your office, and everything outside it belonged to us. What is going on now started with those few extra late nights months ago. It has become more and more. You know it's true. And now these last few weeks, you've been here all night...once or twice? Every night, Kolya, you're a husband. And a father."

He nodded slowly. "This is the last time for a while. I promise."

"Sweetheart, it's almost the end of October. Stasya finishes kindergarten in May. The weeks are going to fly by. Realistically, we need to be settled on a new school in a month or two so that we can begin looking for a new apartment near it in the spring. We have to assume it will take a few months before we can move in. We can't get caught with the school year starting, and, here we are, commuting across the whole of Moscow to take her and pick her up. And I do not want her beginning the year here. I mean the kindergarten was fine, but I don't want her in the primary school here. She needs a school with a good English program. Some native-speaking kids and teachers. I don't want her to have an accent when she speaks English."

"That's why I thought we had decided on a private school. One of the international ones."

"She is Russian. I still want her to have a Russian education, Kolya." She paused, and then continued with a wry smile, "Besides, if she is around rich kids all day, she'll turn into a snob. She'll be impossible by the time she is a teenager. And if she is anything like the women in your family, she'll be difficult to handle anyway."

"Yeah, yeah, it's *your* Cossack outlaw ancestors who were stubborn and defiant," Nikolai said, snuggling her neck.

She gasped and hit him playfully. "Georgians were never Cossacks. I've told you!"

"Anyway," she continued, "there is a perfect school in *Fruzenskaya*. Walks through the parks along the river bank. The cinemas and stores. What do you think? I'll show you the website." She pushed him back so he would have to look up, and her fingers ran across his shirt collar to where it disappeared under his sweater as if to hold him in place.

Nikolai chuckled, but was serious. "No doubt there are a few excellent schools in *Fruzenskaya*. But don't they all have an expensive entry *donation* each year? Honey, the real problem with that area is that we would be lucky to find an apartment even same size as this one, and we would be paying double the rent. Think about it: 150,000 rubles a month when the drop in oil prices drives inflation. I'm not going to get another raise again anytime soon. We're better off staying here than living under those conditions. What about something in *Barrikadnaya?*"

"Too many Americans," she replied in a tone of mild antipathy, shaking her head with an exaggerated frown. "I don't want her around more capitalists like her father. Look what they've done to you." They both laughed a little. She continued, "But school 1950 is near the zoo and would be perfect—both French and English. Anastasia could take her poor old parents to Paris one day." She smiled.

"Well," Nikolai said, "in any case, we would have to move into the city center. That's major money, obviously."

His wife agreed. "And if we have to pay for her school, even with my income, you'll still be working more than you do now. If things continue the way they have been these last three months, she would have a great education but be resentful for the rest of her life because her father was never around."

"We'll manage just fine," he replied. But in truth he knew it would be thornier than that. He was barely making the kind of money now that they needed for the move. There was no margin for mistake or, worse, simply bad luck.

"See, Kolya, these are the conversations we need to have...now. I don't want to make these decisions on my own. She needs both parents. She needs her father. *I* need her father. You're gone as soon as we wake up; you're out until we are asleep; and then you are gone on the weekends, like the past few weeks.... this isn't a family."

Nikolai sighed. "I know. You're right. It's the last time. But I *must* go out tonight."

"You must, you must..." His way of answering had unsettled her. "Where does this vague compulsion come from?" Her words were even more firm when she didn't raise her voice.

"Be straight with me, Nikolai." She uttered the next sentence with such clarity and nonchalance that he did not know how to react. "Have you taken a mistress yet? Is that what this is all about?"

"What? *What?*" He was...astonished, at both the substance and form of the question.

"It's the fashion now, isn't it? Well, it has always been the fashion, but the subtle *openness* of it now is all cosmopolitan and European. Very modern, very chic. Modern Russians for a modern Russia. I watch the

TV dramas and the movies. Look at the best sellers in the bookstores: Adultery is sexy now. All of these women, walking around and thinking the characters that entertain them are based on people other than themselves. They believe that their marriages are somehow different. That they're different. I'm not so easily deluded."

The words *taken* and *yet* still echoed in his ears. *Taken* and *yet*? As if she expected it. As if infidelity was inevitable. His mind raced to catch up.

All he could reply was, "I have no idea what you are talking about."

He lied. It was the first time he had ever truly, irreparably lied to her.

She placed her head on his shoulder and almost whispered as she said carefully, "Kolya, I love you so much, but I'm not an idealist. You know that. We're going to be together for a very long time. We're partners in this marriage and we're parents. I know our love—our physical as well as emotional love—has been cooler in the last year. For both of us. It's natural, it seems. Our romance will ebb and flow over the years. And I know businessmen like you are around temptations every day. Desire fuels capitalism. And you're becoming a very successful capitalist."

He was shaking his head by this point, but she continued calmly, surgically, "The only thing our marriage can't handle is secrets. I cannot handle secrets. The constant insecurity. We can *manage* anything else, especially the temporary undesirable things of life that occur anyway. All that I ask is that you must tell me. And you must still be a father and a husband. Especially a father. I do not want the details, but we must be honest and open. Otherwise you'll crush me, and I know you don't want to hurt me, even when you cheat with another woman now."

She had done it. In her effort to balance everything, she had pushed him into a frenzy of emotions and turmoil. He was churning inside.

What does she know? How?

He had been staring at the ceiling as she spoke, trying to collect himself. But he lowered his stare, surprised at the still-caring, calm look in her eyes.

"Are you finished?" he asked, although he did not wait for her reply. "All these years. That's the worst thing you've ever said to me. How could you be so mean? So cruel?"

She started to speak, but he kept going.

"Look at me. Look at all of me. Everything. I belong to you and Stasya. There is nothing more, no one else." He shook his head. "I don't want a lover. I don't want to be like these people you talk about. I only want the two of you in my life. Even now, these things I do—the work—I do it because they provide the things you both deserve. All of these things cost money. That's fine. I want to give them to you. But I don't enjoy the work like you think. My only real pleasures in this life are my wife and my little girl. These are the only things I love. Nothing else, I tell you. And now you want to talk about *managing* a lover. How dare you!" Nikolai took a deep breath, surprised at himself and barely able to contain the mixture of emotions running through what felt like his entire body. He was dizzy.

Silence.

"Then what's tonight? What are all these late nights about?"

Tonight. The word brought Nikolai back into focus. He had been staring into the nothingness of the tile floor. He looked up at her. He rubbed his forehead and said quietly, as if restoring himself with his own words, "It is a meeting."

This was not completely false.

"Another meeting?" she asked.

"Yes, another meeting." With this topic he was more comfortable. He had an answer ready, carefully worded. "There are other time zones, honey. Somewhere in the world, always, someone important is awake. I have to be on these conference calls to interpret the financial projections. There's a special project that has started. We've been bringing in new personnel who I have to train. This is the price of my promotion last year. But it's almost done. I promise things will be back to normal soon. Believe me, I only want to be here with you."

She wrapped her arms around him. "Kolya, Kolya. You're a good man. I want my good man back." She kissed his cheek and nuzzled her head in his neck again. After a moment she looked at him again and smiled, but he could see her eyes had moistened and were swollen in that deeply natural way. "Stay here. Make love to me. Make love to me tonight."

For a moment, the briefest moment, he considered it. For longer, he wanted to. But reflex overtook him, and he shook his head before the words began: "I cannot. I'm sorry. I have to go now."

"Call in sick. A man is ill from time to time. They must understand that. You have dozens of people working under you. Call one of them. Just for tonight."

He touched her face. "I'm the only one who can do this. There's no one else."

Those words settled the matter. She wiped her eyes, dabbing at her almost tears. Her face regained its resolve. She stood up.

"Then go," she said flatly. She took his plate, knife, and fork from the table and walked toward the sink.

Nikolai pushed the chair back and was startled to see Stasya sitting on the living room floor just outside the door to the kitchen. His first instinct was to wonder how long she had been sitting there, but he knew it could not have been long.

"Anastasia Nikolayevna Tarasova, what are you doing out of bed?" he said as he walked across the room and scooped her up.

She was still sleepy and rubbed her eyes. "I heard you talking, Daddy, and I wanted to see you."

He laughed a little but felt pained as he ran one hand through her baby-blonde hair and carried her across the living room into the corner that was also her bedroom. "My baby girl can always see me. But now you need your sleep."

"What are you and Mommy arguing about?"

"We're not really arguing, baby."

She looked up at him as he laid her back in bed. In the lazy creeping light from the kitchen, she had her mother's eyes with their vibrant shimmer.

"I love you, Daddy."

"I love you too. So much, baby. Now go back to sleep."

"Can we go see the cats on Saturday?"

He smiled. The Moscow Cat Theatre. So innocent to be occupied by simple things. "That's a good idea. Yes, baby, we can go see the cats together. I am sorry I've not been here much lately. Daddy has to work so much right now. We'll definitely spend the whole day together this weekend."

"I love you, Daddy," she said again. For such a solid and sturdy man, his body ached feebly with guilt.

Nikolai tried to think of something to say. But nothing came out except, "Sweet dreams now."

He kissed her forehead. And lingered just a moment as he stood up and pulled the curtain around her bed again. Returning to the kitchen, he collected his coat and shoes.

Nikolai pushed his arms into the sleeves as he watched her open the furthest of the cabinets above the sink and bring down an ashtray, a pack of cigarettes, and a lighter. Everything was clean and put away now. The room had fallen silent. She opened one of the narrow windows in the corner and lit a cigarette. She inhaled. She exhaled. The darkness outside and the angle of the window gave him an almost perfect and vibrant reflection of her: the softness of her face and her beauty. The occasional curvature of her lips around the cigarette. The smoke blowing out the window. But her stare was dark and distant, even though he knew she was looking back at him in the window.

He stood silent. For tonight he was bound to something he could neither alter nor escape. There was nothing in the middle with which he could appease her or assuage her with in the meantime.

Hurry up and get going.

Nikolai stepped forward and placed his hands gently on her lower back. He leaned in and kissed her cheek. She didn't move.

"Tatyana, I love you. More than anything." Then he added, "I'll be home in a few hours."

Starring out the window, she said nothing and merely raised her head in a bit as a nod. Nikolai turned, left the room, and walked through the small apartment to the door.

She heard the latch open and then close behind him. A feeling of emptiness fell over her. She never looked back as he walked away, never tried to stop him, and never said a word. It was something she would regret every day thereafter.

CHAPTER 2

The iron-framed and worn concrete stairs bellowed loudly off the crumbling plaster hallway as Nikolai barreled down them. At the bottom floor, he passed under the checkered shadow of a cobweb hanging between a naked bulb and the wall as he reached for the door handle and stepped outside. The apartment building was considered too old to be outfitted with a numerical keypad and magnetic lock. There was no button to push, just the handle with a loose latch below. So it was with the old *Khrushchyovki* estates.

Nikolai felt the crunch of icy sludge under his boot. The temperature had been shifting back and forth throughout the afternoon and into the evening as the cloud cover came and went. Some scattered patches of grass were layered in fine, slightly impure snow. But the sidewalks had not so easily surrendered their little remaining warmth in the concrete. The flurries had fallen, melted, frozen, and, after being trampled and crushed, they froze again. Somewhat miraculously, the icy mix was mostly still white and only beginning to show the inevitable browning from the mud below.

Nikolai crossed the common yard with its pieces of jungle gyms that had fallen into disrepair. Once they had been colorful, vibrant, and filled with neighborhood children at dusk. Nothing had been replaced since, at least, the early 1990s, and all of those children, who had memories of playing in this courtyard, had long since grown up. The rubber seats of the swings had rotted and disappeared; the paint had cracked and fallen off; and any remaining sturdy bits of metal had long been whisked away in the middle of nights gone by whenever someone had needed scrap.

He glanced back up at his kitchen window as he walked. The light was still on, but Tatyana had disappeared. Then he looked around at the pale-amber, glowing patchwork of windows in all four apartment blocks. A few had elegant chandeliers that seemed to outsize the rooms they were in. Even though the apartment complex was not low-income housing, the ostentatious displays were sour to him as awkward overreaches of upper-middle-class status in order to offset the aged and shabby building exteriors. Nevertheless, vacated apartments were occupied again within days due to their prime location between central Moscow and the suburbs, despite only month-to-month leases because all four buildings would be gone without a trace by the end of the following year.

Not many outsiders realized that the city of Moscow experienced a profound population boom during the 20th century: from 1 million to nearly 11 million in eighty years. Shortly after the 1917 Revolution, the number of new Muscovites began to spike. After World War II, the line on a population chart of the city was completely vertical. The growth had become particularly acute in the 1950s as a result of Stalin's industrialization. This exponential influx of urban population set off a housing crisis.

In the early 1960s, Khrushchev ordered another massive wave of housing construction so that each Soviet family would reap a seemingly inconsistent benefit of victorious Communism: their own exclusive, personal space. Khrushchev actively distanced himself from Stalin's "excesses," and the criticism extended into architecture. The new apartment estates were lauded in the press as a stroke of genius for their simple practicality. Two rooms and a kitchen. "Proletarian housing for a robust proletariat," they editorialized.

The speed at which the apartments were to be erected and the resulting cost were monumental undertakings. Cheap construction methods, cheaper materials. The *Khrushchyovki* were built from prefabricated concrete panels made in city factories, assembled on site, and covered by bland, brown brick with signature red stripes at the top and bottom. One five-story solid rectangle after another appeared because Soviet standards only required elevators in buildings six floors and higher.

The *Khrushchyovki* were designed for thirty-five years of use, at most, by which time they would have been replaced by much better housing indicative of the rapidly nearing realization of the Communist ideal. Party officials had stood at podiums, pounding their fists in the air and stirring the crowds: "The exploitation of the working class might put a car in every garage of some Americans, but in the USSR there will be a roof over every head!" Housing was tangible propaganda.

More than half a century later, those roofs leaked and the *Khrushchyovki* apartment buildings were, indeed, all finally scheduled for demolition to make way for new more modern housing developments. The city planners viewed the *Khrushchyovki* as warts upon cosmopolitan neighborhoods, especially in the nation's capital. They were sore reminders of the frugal illusions of the past and would be replaced by luxury villas, towers of townhouses, or, at minimum, "simple and practical" three- and four-bedroom, two-bath apartments with designer kitchens and spacious living rooms.

Meanwhile, repairs to the *Khrushchyovki* were few and painfully slow. This was probably intentional to encourage the current tenants to relocate, as Tatyana had suggested to Nikolai.

Thus, the Tarasov family was more or less being evicted gently. However, finding something new and respectable in Moscow was financially suffocating.

How do people afford necessities anymore? Moreover, how could an honest person make enough money to do better than just break even?

Nikolai had lain awake at night asking himself these questions, even though he knew the answers, because he also knew a few people his age doing quite well. Connections. Bids for corporate purchasing that somehow beat out better competition. Investments a bit too lucky. Mysterious gifts to those with friends and family in government positions. Corruption in everything but name. In this way, Moscow had entered the league of London, Paris, Beijing, Rome, Washington, and most cities where wealth and government comingle.

Modern Russians for modern Russia. Nikolai chuckled as he walked, remembering Tatyana's words.

The dirt path from the apartment complex to the subway parking lot was well-worn with travel. Occasionally, new gravel was scattered, but most of it disappeared within a few months. On rainy days and nights, such as this one, people were forced into comical zigzag dances around the low-lying areas of the path where small puddles of water and mush formed. At rush hour, those wearing expensive designer shoes could be identified by the extra effort of their leaps.

Nikolai remembered one morning a few months ago when there had been an especially slow moving queue of people crowding the walkway in both directions, waiting to join the puddle-jumping dance. An older man, wearing a newsboy hat and holding a cane, turned around and mused to Nikolai, a complete stranger, "Who do you think will have a happier morning: those who jump or those who splash straight on through?"

At first Nikolai brushed off the question as an eccentric elderly rambling, but moments later, the old man seemed to answer his own question. He attempted a few feeble jumps to and fro, nearly losing his balance each time. He stopped and peered down at his scuffed, worn loafers, looked back up, and flashed a whimsical smile at Nikolai. Then he simply plodded directly through the puddles. A flustered woman, coming from the other way and trying to jump around him, was met with a tip of his hat and a "Good morning, madam."

Nikolai reflected on the old man's Zen as he walked into his office building with his own leather Allen Edmonds shoes still mostly gleaming. Nevertheless, Nikolai stepped over to the soft rotating polisher in the building's lobby anyway, so that his shoes would be spotless and his muddy commute erased.

Tonight, however, Nikolai wore his city boots and did not need to be so careful. He moved down the path instinctively needing no light reflecting on the snow sludge.

Instead, his thoughts were forty-five minutes into the future, to the moment he would get his life back. The apartment lights behind him grew increasingly faint until they mostly faded into darkness and an eerie stillness where the path cut narrowly through the white birch trees. Coming out on the other side of that momentary purgatory, he looked up and saw the blindingly bright luminescence of the street lamps surrounding the metro station in the distance, like a fully lit football stadium misplaced in the middle of a wilderness.

Nikolai stepped onto the solid ground of the nearly empty parking lot and pressed toward the circular, pale-marble subway building. The structure had a shy presence despite the blazing-red outline of the letter *M* on top of it. Since the 1930s, that particular design of the glowing guidepost letter had commanded singular attention like beaming Klieg searchlights throughout Moscow.

Now, despite enduring symbolic nostalgia, this particular *M* was dwarfed by a billboard bolted to the roof of the station, which currently advertised a luxury sports car speeding across a blurred background of organic colors and trailed by the phrase: "*Petrovaryagi*: Fueling Russia, Fueling the World." It was an advertisement for his employer. It made him sick.

To his left a lively conversation was taking place between a man working in a tobacco-and-news shack and his lingering, intoxicated customer. On the ground next to the newsstand stood a wooden A-frame sign affixed with a headline soon to expire at midnight in the *Moskovskij Komsomolets:* "White October!"

The little shop was open twenty-four hours, the only place alive around the subway station at this time of night. It also formed the anchor from which the bare framework of half-a-dozen market stalls radiated outward. Although deserted after 9:00 p.m. and merely shells with the occasional rotting crate or torn empty box laying around, during the day, the area bustled with people hurriedly shooting in different directions on their way home with small stuffs of vegetables, fruits, bread, nuts, fish, herbs, and meat.

Nikolai passed the same busy market every morning and evening. It had become a vivid fixture in his routine. In fact, his imagination now summoned each character back into their rightful places like a crooked chain of ghosts.

Tonight, Nikolai walked among those ghosts more than he realized.

The customers, who had been just momentary passersby, left only a slight memory mark and were merely silhouettes in his mind: they were surreal forms, slowly floating around the stalls and drifting back toward the woods and their apartments and families.

But Nikolai recalled every detail of the sellers' faces. First, there was the bald man about Nikolai's age with the booming voice, who sang opera while selling fish. Next, around the high stacks of vegetables, was an unkempt couple, working in tandem and constantly arguing with each other until a customer stepped up to their stall.

And then there were the shelves of herbs and spices in the space between the fish and produce stalls. For years, an old hunchbacked gypsy woman had hovered over the boxes containing those smells and tastes. Whether snow, rain, wind, or sweltering heat, she was there every morning and evening in clothes that rarely changed with the seasons. She looked so frail, but she could shuttle around in that small cube of space, instantly conjuring a genuine, if etched, smile while handing over a small plastic bag with a few scoops of herbs or spice—like a sorceress who had given up the dark arts and been rehabilitated into more mundane work.

Nikolai had not purchased anything from her, but every day she noticed him walk by and gave him a nod. The old woman never tried to tempt him toward a sale but merely acknowledged him. He did not see her give the same nod to anyone else, and it made him feel somewhat special among the commuters. He would nod to her in reply, sometimes with a slight wave. The habit and gravity of the rush hour had always nudged Nikolai along without stopping, although every so often, he made a mental note to pause someday soon and buy something from her.

The years rolled by and he never actually purchased any herbs or spices, but their relationship continued with the mutual nods. Maybe he sensed that making it any more personal would have broken her spell.

Then, one afternoon about two years ago, Nikolai exited the subway on his way home and immediately sensed something was out of place. As he neared the market, one of the stalls was empty, void of person or product. The surrounding ones were full and busy as usual, but there was a gap, as though one had been suddenly and utterly abandoned.

Nikolai drew closer to the spice stall than he had ever been before. Where rows of small boxes of herbs and spices had once sat, now only a single flower remained. It was a ruffled rose blossom with a yellow-cream center that blended increasingly pink as the petals folded outward. Nikolai had never seen another flower like it.

He stood still for a moment in disbelief, trying to locate the old woman elsewhere. *Surely he had confused the order of the stalls today*, he thought. *Vegetables on one side, fish on the other, and in the middle should be...* He looked around. *Perhaps she had just moved, but all the other stalls were the same, and nothing was out of place.*

A certain realization set in and something vanished in Nikolai, too, leaving him with an inner void. He drifted a few steps backward, took a last look at the pink blossom, and then scratched his head as he turned and set out among the birch trees toward home.

Three days later, the stall was full of the same boxes of herbs and spices again. But now two teenage girls were behind the counter. Like the old woman, both appeared to be gypsies. Nikolai rushed over and pulled some change out of his pocked to buy something. The two girls welcomed him warmly as he asked for some thyme and a bit of ginger. Both listened to his order, and one of them started to fill it, while the other looked over his shoulder to the customer behind him. The young girl fumbled a bit as she hurriedly scooped the shaved ginger into a small plastic bag. Nikolai watched closely and noticed that she was blind, or nearly so. But her following attempt with the thyme was more confident.

Nikolai said, "The two of you are new. There are so many different boxes that it must be tricky to choose the correct one so quickly."

She replied with a smile, tensing the side of her face while taking his money, counting it by feel, and handing him two small bags. "I am getting faster. When we open in the mornings, it is just matter of making sure each box is where it is supposed to be."

Nikolai thanked her and started to turn away.

"But I think I might have to switch them around a bit every few days," she added with a small laugh, "to make sure I don't get bored."

He stopped by once or twice a week thereafter, and she had indeed grown faster and more efficient. Possibly even more so than the old woman had been.

Ghosts.

The word brought Nikolai back into the reality of the present moment as he reached the threshold of the door of *Vladykino* subway station, stomped the snow from his feet, and ran his ticket through the turnstile. Because it was late in the evening, he was alone on the escalator as it descended.

A subway train had just arrived. Nikolai broke into a trot and entered the blue carriage car a moment before the doors closed behind him. It was almost empty, and he took a seat while raising his sleeve to check his watch. He would arrive just after 23:30. Late but acceptable.

Nikolai leaned back in his seat as the train accelerated and looked at his surroundings. The space in the subway carriage seemed hollow with only five other people. A few seats away, two young men sat with a girl between them. She was striking due to the long, white-silk Amelia Earhart scarf below her freckled faced and brightly dyed crimson hair.

The two guys were a contrast: One had spiked, purple-tipped hair and face piercings; he wore black skinny jeans and a black-leather coat over a T-shirt with the letter *A* inside a circle. His was a punk look. The other had a military flattop haircut, '80s oval eyeglasses, torn jeans, brown-leather shoes, and a green woodsman vest over a white T-shirt. They were obviously coming from a party.

She was flirting with both of them, her hand on the flattop's leg, while leaning in close and talking loudly to the punk. The former was quiet and his face was blank. The punk alternated between texting and agreeing with everything she said, all of which seemed incoherent to Nikolai. Again and again, the punk's ringtone screeched bluntly. The girl glanced across at Nikolai every few minutes and gave him quick coy smiles. He tried paying her no attention, but she never took the hint.

To Nikolai's right, at the far end of the subway car and sleeping against its back wall, was a middle-aged man with a central-Asian look about him and a young boy of about ten asleep on his lap. A tattered and stained backpack, heaving with clothes and small items, was tucked under the man's arm. Nikolai figured they were riding the subway in circles to avoid the weather and get whatever rest possible until they were kicked off.

Even from this distance, Nikolai could see the man's sedate glazed eyes and his drooping eyelids. He tilted a liquor bottle up a few times and swallowed the booze as he ran his other hand through the boy's hair. Then he placed the empty bottle on the floor and spun it around in a circle. As the bottle slowed, it started rolling to the other end of the car and picked up speed as the subway began to brake for the next stop. A sweet stench wafted in front of Nikolai when the bottle passed by him and then rolled under a seat.

Two stops later at *Mendeleyevskaya,* the two guys and the girl exited. Nikolai was left alone with the silent, almost nonexistent man and boy at the rear. The doors closed with a *ping*, and the subway train was soon back at full speed.

Nikolai watched the car in front bounce and twist as they rushed along, and, again, it felt unnatural to be in solitude in that space. Just as he had done in the market, he filled the car with rush-hour ghosts who stood out in his memory: a collection of some colorful and unusual souvenirs collected over time. Now, he brought them together into a single ride.

There was the smelly and greasy long-haired tramp who entered through the doors with a dented cage of stuffed birds. He walked down the aisle with his hat in hand, whistling different bird calls with surprising talent. Not one coin was placed in his hat as he stopped every few steps. As the tramp angled to move to the next car, he bumped into a smartly dressed man who turned his head and gave the cage a disgusted look.

Then the well-dressed man turned to the guy standing with him and began to speak scathingly of the cage in emphatic sign language evidence by his scowl and gestures. The other man, who apparently was not deaf but understood sign language, wore white earphones that dipped into his coat and held a blue shopping bag with thirteen yellow stars encircling the word *Evropeisky*. He calmly looked back and held the bag up higher in an effort to respond with both hands, which must have produced an effect similar to talking while chewing. Visibly relaxed, the first man nodded, touched his friend's arm, and leaned in. The two men kissed lovingly. The blue bag was lowered again and hung near a mother sitting next to her daughter. While the woman knitted, the little girl rocked her feet back and forth as they hung off the seat.

Across from the young girl sat an elderly woman, who Nikolai deduced, apparently had cataracts because, although her grandmotherly hair was fixed neatly, it had a blue tint. He remembered that his own grandmother had the same blueness about hers. Nikolai's father had once explained she was using a diluted dye in an attempt to give her gray hair a shine. However, because she also had cataracts, she could not see lighter shades of the color blue and overdyed it, thinking it was a fine silver sheen instead.

Being stubbornly independent, his grandmother refused to allow anyone do the dyeing for her, and so she walked around oblivious to her blue hair for fifteen years because no one could bring themselves to tell her otherwise. When she was buried, the family had a surprisingly prolonged debate over whether the mortician should color her hair correctly or not. The blue faction won out. However, the undertaker himself was not an expert in this area, and a young Nikolai remembered watching the casket close on what, to him, seemed like a sleeping circus clown, much to his amusement and satisfaction. He laughed at the memory even now.

The young girl, perplexed by the sight of a blue-haired woman across from her, watched her intently. When the woman noticed the girl's attention, she popped her dentures out of her mouth, held them in her hand, and flashed a toothless grin. It seemed to Nikolai that the woman was merely trying to amuse the girl, but the combination of spitting out a full set of teeth against a backdrop of blue hair was too much of a shock. She burst into tears, hiding her face against her mother, who looked up and saw the scene, patted her head, and kept knitting.

The subway came to a halt. The doors opened and, still, no one entered the carriage. But for Nikolai, it emptied of some ghosts and then filled up again with other apparitions. He recalled the wheels of a polka-dotted baby carriage rocking clumsily into the subway car. It was being pushed by a man in a black turtleneck and a wild retro sports jacket, who fumbled with getting the pram into the corner and locking the wheel brake. After exhaling, the man jerked upward, reached inside his jacket, and produced a small writing pad and pen. He began scrawling as he stood there.

This was a rather mundane image, and Nikolai wondered why he remembered it at all. It probably stuck with him because it seemed an odd preface to the following moments.

Behind the man as he scribbled, an elderly woman with a cane shuffled in with great effort and cleared the doors just before they closed. She had reached such an age that Nikolai could not have been able to guess how old she really was. Dressed in a light-brown sweater and a charcoal-gray, loose, woolen skirt to her knees, showing her varicose-veined lower legs and swollen ankles, she held onto the carriage wherever she could, using her cane as balance, as the subway lunged forward.

Like the tramp before her, she moved down the aisle, but frailly and slowly. Again and again, she repeated her own bird call, "Excuse me."

But the professional and stylish passengers moved aside begrudgingly and as little as possible. *Had there not been enough space for her to stay near the door?* their expressions asked. Past the fully occupied seats she went with no one paying much attention and sometimes deliberately so. One young man fidgeted as though he were in a crisis of conscience about whether or not to stand up for her. His hesitation lingered until she had already passed by, and he remained in his seat with a look of relief.

A few steps before she reached Nikolai, a darker-skinned man with a white beard and a karakul hat, who had been texting on his phone, looked up and stood quickly. He waved her into his seat. "Please, here, please," he said in accented Russian.

He helped her lower into the seat. When she was settled, she reached up and patted his hand and lightheartedly replied, "I've been looking everywhere for you, my dear."

But the one person who stood out most vividly to Nikolai, as he moved from memory to memory, was a woman of obvious extreme wealth dressed from head to toe in shamrock green. Her green coat covered a green sweater, both of which matched her trousers and shoes. And to top it off, a green 1920s cloche hat tilted on her head. In fact, the only things *not* green about her were small golden spectacles (too small to be considered eyeglasses) sitting low on her nose and a white magazine cover titled in English: *Condé Nast Traveler.* She never took her eyes off it, even as she exited the subway car.

Despite all the individual ghosts in his mind, tonight it was just Nikolai, the man, and the boy. He looked back down the carriage; they had scarcely moved.

Each cylinder of the Moscow Metro is a modern congress of Russia. The almost rich, the mostly homeless, and those scattered in-between are all funneled together down into the tunnels below the capital city. The ugly and the beautiful. Intelligentsia next to the unlettered. Fine suits and heelless socks. The manicured and the unwashed. Leathery wrinkles and the scarcely born. It is a place where employees can sit and the employers will stand.

Every kilometer of the country is represented, as well as the farthest corners of the former Soviet empire. One by one they ticket through to a space where they elbow and heave as equals, regardless of ability or need. And together they are shoved, rattled, and tossed off balance on top of grimy floors and in the stale air of the finest subway in the world. Nikolai had been born a Muscovite. This subway ran through him like his veins—a flowing and curving community—and he did not like to be alone in its catacombs.

Almost reflexively, eight million daily commuters watched someone else for a few seconds but rarely really saw them. And, in their finest moments of overcrowded, hot, and annoying rush hours, all were touching but few were touched. Nikolai agonized that while these were intrinsically intimate meetings of people, they were increasingly distant encounters. The isolation of earphones, the tapping of smart phones, the thumb scrolls of e-books, and the sharp pen strokes of Sudoku encouraged a silence of self-absorption. Even companions tended to whisper among themselves. Sure, the odd puncture of raucous laughter, the booming ringtone, the babble of a troubled mind or soul, a roaming jester, and most often a baby's cry could be heard. But they were simply endured with a tenor of perturbation.

As a child when personal technological luxuries were nonexistent, Nikolai's memories of the adults sitting around him in antiquated subway carriages were of strangers endlessly griping and grumbling to each other. But it was to *each other* they vented their futile, indirect dissatisfactions. Now, it seemed to Nikolai, the travelers defied this cylinder of human connectivity by carving a corner of the world for themselves alone. And as part of Moscow's modernization, Wi-Fi was installed throughout the subway system so passengers would never be out of touch with their virtual selves. Even the older generations had mostly grown silent because when attempting to speak to someone younger next to them, the person being spoken to would turn their head away as if the friendly words were contagious babbles of dementia.

The nothingness of so many people shoulder to shoulder staggered him. The swivel of wind around the shell of the car, the broken clacks, and sudden brakes were all that remained, until, finally, the inner silence was pierced by a crackling voice.

"Now approaching *Chekhovskaya. Chekhovskaya* next stop."

Nikolai thought that, if little else, the Communists did one thing perfectly: They had built the stations of the Moscow Metro to be opera houses and cathedrals for the common women and men. Stalin himself had commissioned and oversaw their original construction in the 1930s, directing the architects to symbolize a collective "radiant future." Each was designed around a different cultural or geographical theme, and, even today, few of the nearly 200 Metro stations are identical.

The grandest among them form a ringed route under the city center. There is *Komsomolskya* with its extravagant Ming-yellow, baroque ceiling and friezes that glorify the fortitude of Russian soldiers in World War II. An image of Lenin speaking to the people on top an explosion of gold, emanating from a blood-red, five-pointed star, sits high above one end of that station.

Ploschad Revolyutsii is infused with a three-dimensional celebration of the proletariat through its seventy-two bronze statutes of farmers, factory workers, and schoolchildren—all sitting among the walls of dark, earthy Armenian marble. There is even one of a guard with a dog, and, if you rub its nose, the statute is believed to bring good luck.

The low, curling passages of *Novoslobodskaya* house sacred narratives of material abundance foretold by illuminated stained glass, which leads to a prodigious mosaic proclaiming "Peace Throughout the World."

The milky-white walls and pink columns of *Belorusskaya* remind Muscovites of rural life and the agricultural contributions to the Revolution made by those toiling in the countryside.

The optical illusions of the temple to electrical engineering, *Elektrozavodskaya*, named for a lightbulb factory nearby, was completed in 1944. Its seemingly never-ending rows of circular-inset lamps are futuristic and otherworldly in their splendor. Excellence in mathematics and sciences under the Soviets was a source of national pride. They not only rocketed Sputnik, the first satellite, into space in 1957, but also the first human being, Yuri Gagarin, in 1961. Three weeks after Gagarin's feat, the USA launched Alan Shepard, but Shepard did not achieve an actual orbit around the Earth like his Soviet counterpart.

And *Paveletskaya* is grandiose for the sheer symmetrical simplicity of its classical marble columns, directing all attention to the cardinal Soviet emblems. Its theme is a nod to the trains departing Moscow toward the Volga River region. The Volga, which meanders through Western Russia and provides fresh water to the major cities between its headspring north of Moscow and its outlet into the Caspian Sea, is longest river in Europe. Russian arts and literature attribute a reverent and almost mythical status to it, often referring to the river as "Mother Volga."

From the Kremlin, their majesty shoots out in all directions: *Prospekt Mira, Avtozavodskaya, Semionovskaya, Oktiabrskaya, Taganskaya, Baumanskaya,* and *Dorbininskaya.* The list goes on, each one a rigorous and inspired work of art from revered architects and artisans throughout the land: "Palaces of the People," gifts for their past steadfast sacrifices in war, harvests of triumphs, and heralds for the days ahead. As they moved across the city together, going about their lives as USSR citizens, they would experience beauty in the subway that usually was only reserved for the elites elsewhere in the world. As Lenin said, "Art has no use unless it serves politics." Most of all, the stations reinforced a narrative and feeling of a national community progressing together, an ultimate inspiring symbol of solidarity. In short, pride through camaraderie.

On most trips, even his bustling commutes to work, Nikolai made a point to stop and admire whichever station he was in for several minutes, absorbing the details as if in a museum.

On the day the first Moscow subway line opened in 1935, his grandparents had persevered through the queues of thousands of people to ride the marvel and be part of the historic festival. When he was about Anastasia's age, Nikolai's grandfather often took him into the city center early in the morning for a modest breakfast, and then the two of them would be standing at the door when the subway opened. Back and forth they would ride it all morning, stopping at each station along the way. He always remembered how his grandfather's wrinkled hand felt when taking his and guiding the young Nikolai between the columns and throughout the caverns as the old man made up stories about whatever mosaic or frieze they admired.

Now when Anastasia traveled with Nikolai, they would also linger on the platforms and corridors. He would tell her the same stories his grandfather had told him and watch her imagination turn a subway into caverns of imaginary wonder, just as his own imagination had done years ago.

But not tonight.

CHAPTER 3

Nikolai stood and moved to the subway door. Its window returned a half reflection and then disappeared in the light of the platform, reminding him of his last view of Tatyana before he had left their apartment.

He exited *Chekhovskaya*, took the escalator up, and turned toward the corridor leading to the adjoining *Tverskaya* station. *Chekhovskaya-Teverskaya*, a major hub for three different lines, normally roared with a flow of dissonant footsteps echoing through the corridors and amplifying down the passageways until spilling over onto a sea of passengers.

But tonight, as if the city itself knew the purpose for Nikolai's meeting, what little sound came from the few people in the station evaporated at the platform opening. For such a large city with so many people and ways to evidence themselves through sound, the mammoth hall was abnormally hushed like an abbey between the end of a Sunday mass and the beginning of a funeral. This unsettling strangeness paralleled his imminent rendezvous with the woman who had ominously entered his life, and if Nikolai had not been utterly unnerved before, he was now.

The next subway car slowed and arrived.

Riding public transport means surrendering oneself to an external constraint. No amount of desire or willfulness can push the vehicle along faster. A passenger, like Nikolai, might be anxious about arriving on time but also experience a calming effect from accepting loss of control over the situation. Being forced to merely endure time is a unique emotion. Nikolai's momentary powerlessness was a respite he used to catch his breath and attempt to refocus.

With his destination, *Teatralnaya*, approaching, Nikolai felt the weight of the moment upon him. He was ready, and he was reconciled to it. He knew he could not turn back.

Or could he? Might he still be able to turn around, or had he already gone too far? Could he ever have turned back once he had met her? At what particular moment did he veer onto the path that had brought him inexorably to this night?

He knew the answers yet continually denied them, desperately hoping for a different result. With a sigh, he closed his eyes and rubbed his temples as he neared the end of this journey to barter for his freedom. Soon he could physically walk away from her, but he could never forget.

Still, the first thing he would do when he got home would be to crawl into bed and wake up Tatyana with his embrace just to lay next to her, stroke her hair, and meet her eyes with less fear and shame. He longed to watch her watching him until he was cleansed and whole—to the extent that he could ever be again. Her eyes affectionately stripped him bare, and he always returned to them. Their penetrating copper-brown color was otherworldly, like something ancient lost in the Middle Ages and only unearthed and rediscovered during the genesis of her soul at birth.

Tatyana's mother was Georgian and her father was a Kazan Tartar. Her parents had first met in the break room of a truck factory, although she rarely spoke of their relationship. But once, a few days before their wedding, as if a warning, Tatyana revealed that her parents had a tempestuous, passionate, and secret beginning because her mother had been engaged to another man. By the time her mother broke off the engagement, she was already pregnant with Tatyana.

Her parents' love maintained a vigorous momentum for about ten years and then cooled. They began to drift, and eventually her father had a series of poorly hidden affairs. Her mother simply refused to acknowledge what everyone else knew and suffered in silence. The festering secret and the cancerous effect it had on her mother pained Tatyana until she simply moved out of their house and distanced herself from her family.

Nikolai knew the mark those feelings had left on her still remained and probably always would.

Only one story stood out in Nikolai's family history. His great-grandfather had been a somewhat well-known bourgeois gardener for the Tsar and his great-grandmother a chambermaid who came from an impoverished family. His great-grandfather had been impressed by the Bolsheviks and joined the movement years before the Revolution. In the Soviet purges that followed, even though his great-grandfather had been associated with the monarchy, his bona fides as a true Communist went unquestioned—not the least because he had effectively "married down" a class, which was unheard of at the time.

Their son, Nikolai's grandfather, had been conscripted into the Soviet Army at the age of sixteen and sent to Stalingrad, where he managed to survive the brutal siege of the city in 1942–43, although he rarely spoke of it, probably due to his survivor's guilt. No one dared ask his grandfather, even during late nights of heavy drinking, how many people he had killed or watched die in the war. In the initial onslaught, the Nazi *Luftwaffe* reduced Stalingrad to rubble. The city ruins became the setting of relentless close-quarter combat from street to street, building to building, and literally room to room—even in the sewers. Each day for more than five months, the Nazis and Soviets ordered waves of soldiers, often at gunpoint, into the cauldron of the combat zone simply to reduce the other's ammunition supply. The life expectancy of an enlisted soldier was less than twenty-four hours and for officers it was three days. Stalin refused to allow city residents, including women and children, to evacuate and instead turned them into last-resort combatants. Eventually, in the dead of a Russian winter, the Soviets encircled the city, trapping the Nazis inside with any remaining Russians. Hitler refused to surrender, and the Soviets were in no mood to take prisoners. Stalingrad turned into a bloodbath; although most of the 2 million causalities in the city were Russian, the loss devastated the Germans. Stalingrad was the turning point of the entire war. The Nazi *Wehrmacht* never fully recovered before the D-Day invasion eighteen months later. All told, the Soviet Union suffered a staggering 27 million casualties throughout the war, as compared to the 1.5 million combined casualties for the USA, UK, and France. Many historians argue that no bloodier or more ferocious single battle was fought in recorded human history than Stalingrad. Due to the military distinction that came from surviving that battle, Nikolai's grandfather soon found work in a large dry goods store upon returning to Moscow. After a few years of living thin and saving, he opened up his own modest store and turned it over to Nikolai's father when the time came.

Unlike Tatyana, Nikolai's childhood had been charmed and uneventful. His parents were loving and boring, and, as the second of three children, he had received both a healthy amount of attention and independence to develop on his own. Nikolai had not excelled like his older sister, nor been much of a troublemaker like his younger brother. Rather, he had been a quiet and stable teenager. He did, however, become fascinated by the logistics of taking inventory in his father's storehouse and ordering replacement stocks of goods.

Nikolai balanced a solid business mind with a captainship of his school's boxing team, impressing the head of his school enough to secure him a place at Moscow State. Although he took a room near the university, Nikolai traveled home every Sunday to have dinner with his parents, and his relationship with them matured fondly as the years went by. Even now after his father and mother had passed on, he still dropped in on his sister's family most Sundays, sometimes with Tatyana and Anastasia and sometimes on his own. But even those visits had lost their priority and fallen by the wayside over the last few months.

A particular memory of his mother increasingly replayed in Nikolai's mind of late. He remembered walking hand in hand with her past a busy expensive restaurant. Being a child around ten years old, it must have been in the late 1970s. His mother stopped and looked in the window briefly. He remembered the abrupt pull on his hand followed by them staring into the shiny glass.

She glanced down at him and said excitedly with a laugh, "Kolya, there was a time when your mother was a young woman and she had wanted to be a gourmet chef in a restaurant like this one. Can you imagine your mother that way? I dreamed of creating art from food in a beautiful sparkling kitchen full of ovens, mixers, and icing twists. From fire to plate with a slight taste before flying away in the hand of a waiter."

The melancholic aura that set in over her face that day became imprinted on Nikolai's memory.

She kneeled down and pulled him close, peering into his eyes. "I tried new things with every meat and vegetable brought through our door in the hope of a place at the best culinary school. But in those days, such a dream did not fit with the jobs that were needed. Your uncle showed promise in math and was chosen to attend university. I was encouraged to be a nurse, and that is what I did until you were born, my dear. But you'll be able to do anything you want. Dream big, Kolya. Things are changing."

Things had indeed changed, but not as his mother had hoped.

The Berlin Wall collapsed during Nikolai's final year of university, followed by the Soviet Union thereafter, just as Nikolai was admitted to new courses on Western business models. He completed an MBA study program at Moscow State, which was a minor revolution in its day, a sudden outgrowth of *Perestroika*.

All things had been possible in the early days of Russia's revival. There was a frenzy of capitalization, ambition, and unrestrained optimism, but the sense of societal possibility and confidence was short-lived.

Nikolai vividly remembered being at a dinner party with Tatyana and a few friends less than a year after the end of Communist governance. A seasoned economist named Pytor, who sat at the head of the table, began to argue politics after a few drinks. It was the first time Nikolai remembered anyone foretelling the decline of Russia and the cracking financial structure of the entire country. Such pessimism was unheard of at the time. The others, Tatyana especially, had looked at him as though he had gone insane.

Pytor's prognostications were prescient. By 1994, Russia's gross domestic product had sunk to thirteenth in the world—behind even Mexico, South Korea, and Italy. Ownership of profitable, formerly state-owned corporations was transferred to a few obscure and well-connected individuals, who generously rewarded the politicians and bankers facilitating the privatization deals. Then they sent their enormous new wealth outside of Russia to Switzerland and London instead of reinvesting. The internal economy collapsed.

Suddenly, basic care and aid were unavailable; the death rate outpaced the birthrate. Prices of normal things increased over 2,000%. In three years the poverty rate had staggeringly increased from 2% to 50% of the Russian population. The shelter of the welfare state had nearly vanished, replaced by the prospect of destitution in the face of personal hardship. The reliability of the police crumbled, leaving people to the whims of various mafias, black markets, and other unknowns. And it all happened so fast. A new conventional wisdom of Russia as a poor, chaotic, second-class power painfully penetrated the national psyche.

Counterrevolution follows revolution, and in true Russian style, the one of the late 1990s had been as harsh as a brutal midwinter. Nikolai was not surprised, and was even somewhat relieved, when people turned to heavy-handed and often ruthless national leaders. Despite these shortcomings, the new guard in the Kremlin reestablished stability and promised rapid economic development to recover from the climate of collective shame and individuals' fears.

But each scrap of stability came at a cost; the new leadership had to pacify both the oligarchs and mafia bosses by making deals with them. Doing so was a rough and messy business, and, as a result, even the well-intentioned leaders became stained and vulnerable to potential persecution by overly enthusiastic political successors. Consequently, the only way to ensure their positions and interests was to maintain a grip on power by becoming the *padrone* and fostering a new, retro aristocracy.

This vague, expansive notion and the phrase "national economic development" seemed to justify everything, but the only quick stimulant was oil and gas. The Russian economy, and, by extension, the near future of its people became chained to an inescapable single-sector addiction. Nikolai knew this all too well because, after finishing his studies, the only attractive job offer came from *Petrovaryagi*, a privatized petroleum company owned by a dependable and malleable oligarch.

Shortly after the Berlin Wall fell in 1989, Nikolai remembered the time with his mother in front of the expensive restaurant that had long since closed, its building in disrepair. By this time, Nikolai was much older and so was his mother. The two of them were out for a walk one afternoon when he asked her whether she had been resentful about not being able to be a chef.

She had shrugged and replied as she kept walking, "Nikolai, in those days we all understood the bargain between us and the government. We would keep to their plan, and they would take care of us."

With that, she had nothing more to say on the subject.

For her birthday that year, he had tightly saved money and gave her some cooking lessons in a new Cordon Bleu school for the public. She had immensely enjoyed the first few sessions until she became ill and died quickly thereafter.

"Now approaching *Teatralnaya*. Next stop *Teatralnaya*."

The station was busy with people travelling the opposite direction, going home after the ballet and theatre performances—thus, the subway stop's name. Nikolai cut through the crowd, leaving them in his wake.

On the banks of the Moskva River, looking back toward the Kremlin, stands the magnificent Cathedral of Christ the Savior. The tallest orthodox cathedral in the world, with its cream stone walls and five golden gilded *zvonnitsas*, it rises over 100 meters into the sky. Originally commissioned in 1812, it took more than sixty years to build, and was the site of the inaugural performance of Tchaikovsky's *1812 Overture*. Less than fifty years after its resplendent Byzantine interior had finally been consecrated, Stalin ordered it dynamited to make way for a new Palace of the Soviets. But after the cathedral had been razed, the project was abandoned and replaced by a swimming pool instead. The amount of rubble was so great that it took months to remove; some of the original stone was whisked away shortly after the demolition and preserved in the catacombs of *Teatralnaya* station. Despite the widespread financial hardship in 1994, more than 1 million Muscovites contributed to a fund to reconstruct a replica of the original structure. The new cathedral was completed and consecrated in an astonishing six years.

It was the last time Nikolai could recall the city unified around an idea.

He finally began ascending to the street and looked around, wondering which pieces of the walls were from the original cathedral. Unlike some, Nikolai had no nostalgia for the former Soviet Union. Far from it. But he acknowledged that the USSR at least provided the Russian people with a national narrative, a coherence. They were all working towards *something* as a *community*. An ideal. A connection with humanity and each other. Even his mother had understood this and borne its weight against her particular dream. The Communist government collapsed simply because the theory did not work in practice, not because people rejected the essential ideals of Soviet society. When that communal narrative imploded and vanished, Nikolai felt a replacement, which defined what it meant to be Russian and also inspired a path toward achieving something *together* as a *people,* had not fully materialized.

Since his childhood, the story of his mother's lost aspirations had turned him into a fierce believer in the innate decency of the freedom to live one's life in a manner that brought individual happiness. But seeing the devastation of the society around him for years, Nikolai recognized that people also crave a larger societal and communal narrative to make sense of their lives, and they feel somewhat lost without it. They do not wish to be dominated by the narrative, rather to sense that their particular life paths have a role and contribution within the bigger picture. People want to live their individual freedoms within the community around them—even if it means rebelling against the "norm" or moving to a new community that suits them better.

But essentially our lives are referenced by others: the artists' interpretations, the doctors who heal, the innovators thinking beyond, the firemen who protect, the religions we choose, the academics' teaching, and so on. Even being a mother or father, introducing a blank slate of a human being to the world, is affected by and has a role in the societal narrative around them.

Without a societal narrative, the gap is filled by an endless narrative of "self": the glorification of personal comforts and wealth in order to provide luxury for family and nearest friends. In general Nikolai would not criticize making money to better one's life experiences, especially for one's family. Our prehistoric ancestors passed along the default instinct of self-interest to us, and while nothing is wrong with self-interest, contemporary self-interest, or personal indulgence, has fewer and fewer natural counterbalances.

When indulgent accumulation underlies daily life, most other people become a means to an end, as opposed to being an end in and of themselves. Why take care of one another? Why be kind and connect with strangers in passing if they have nothing to offer you financially?

Nikolai's colleagues began to talk exclusively about money, luxury goods, and the desires of their families. And when they were not talking about themselves, they were asking about his money and the desires of his family. Once he entered the business world, he took his cue from the higher echelons and gradually became increasingly focused on his personal wealth and the future of his family's lifestyle. This was the actual measure of success for those around him.

Other people must fend for themselves; they were not his responsibility. He had rationalized it over and over again. With more property, more possessions, more access to exclusive locations, the need for others and a community with its inconveniences could be left behind. Nikolai was never vicious or mean in temperament. He never raised his voice to anyone. In fact, he was different than his colleagues in many ways: always gentle and kind to strangers around him. But he was also a practical man. It was the respectable way of life. His family deserved luxuries.

The more Nikolai watched Anastasia, the more his new conflicting feelings crystalized and weighed on him. Not only because of the environment she was growing up in, but because every time they talked about moving her to a prestigious school, it reminded him that she desperately needed it to eventually secure her own financial prosperity. Her education must set her apart and ensure her superiority, because nothing or no one else would give her a second chance or help her along. The status of her elite education really was everything, and it was a costly, nonnegotiable commodity in today's world. The wealthy purchased it with little thought. Those who surely could not afford such institutions reconciled their lot in life, moved on, and made the most of it.

The real "victims" were the parents, like Nikolai and Tatyana, who could *almost* afford it if they denied themselves most comforts. Tatyana had once compared their situation to fasting, but Nikolai reminded her that fasting was a choice and could be broken. He shivered at the consequences of only being able to send Anastasia to a mediocre school.

About a year ago, he looked around on the subway one day and realized that most people had now subconsciously internalized the same idea: personal wealth and family luxury to the exclusion of everyone else. Recognizing this evolution pained Nikolai when he rode his beloved Moscow subway.

He had been born a Russian and a Muscovite. There was a time when that had meant something uncommon, but any sense of loyalty or communal unity had now become the rarest of all luxuries. People rode the subways, they walked the streets, and so few gave a thought about each other for more than a moment. They were busy.

Every day Nikolai saw examples of suffering people on the subway. Some acutely, like the drunken man and his boy and the tramp making bird sounds for money. Others just a little, like the older woman looking for an empty seat. Nikolai realized that people did not wish anyone misfortune, illness, or injustice on others. It was just that more and more of them felt too hurried and too removed from the suffering of others to take any responsibility for it, like the two men who spoke in sign language or the girl in the scarf.

This was not intentional, but a more a subliminal self-absorption, which made the subway Wi-Fi such a welcome, although ruinous, improvement. The Internet and social networks could bring people thousands of miles away closer than the person actually sitting next to them. And now "people" seemed to increasingly mean "me" or a very narrow "us." All too often, these tailor-made, technological self-spaces left little room for empathy beyond a fleeting and passive nature.

Nikolai realized that when community relationships starved and withered, it led to deeper dark consequences that he had not grasped until it was too late.

Moscow had once been the epicenter of at least the dream of equality. But now, as in many economies across the globe, profit at any cost had become sacred. Anything to increased profit was justified these days. And when something hindered the accumulation of greater wealth, a roomful of clever lawyers and accountants sat down and calculated the potential cost of damages versus the profit at stake.

Nikolai was one of those accountants.

Everything and everyone has a price, literally. It is a statistical fact that an airplane will drop from the sky, killing everyone on board, every once in a while. But, ultimately, airlines make more money than they pay out to victims' families, and air travel is good for society. Therefore, society can stomach the grim economics because if an airplane carrying hundreds of people crashes, it is usually an accident. This calculus is applied widely. Massive oil spills. Nuclear power plant leaks. Exploding gas tanks in cars. Risky pharmaceuticals. In all such instances, the decisive question, a sort of morality in its own right, is whether something produces more profit than human cost. Or, more accurately, if there is an accident, will it cost more to clean up the catastrophe than to make a profit?

But what if there were no accident? What if someone calculated the profit to be made by actively ending a certain number of human lives? Deliberately. Knowingly.

Nikolai knew.

He watched it happen, vaguely sensed something was wrong, but said nothing until after it had been done. He could have asked questions, but he did not. In fact, not only he was a complicit silent bystander, he later realized that he had kept the financial ledgers and paid the bills that made it possible.

The ability to prevent the foreseeable suffering of another human being, yet choosing not to, can be a form of pure greed if it is clearly a profit-based decision. However, the most sinister greed is often more subtle, such as when the resulting human misery is presented as a "necessity," although it is really expedient. Essentially, truly venal greed is disguised as "for the greater good."

A few months ago, some pieces of otherwise unremarkable paper had been placed on Nikolai's desk. Yet as he perused them, the numbers, though obscure, eventually revealed something horrific. In fact, it was those papers that had brought him from the warmth of his apartment into this particular frosty Moscow night.

As he pushed through the door and exited the subway, a woman stopped to light a cigarette in mid-step almost before she was outside. It took great effort for Nikolai to catch himself, pivot, and narrowly avoid knocking her over. As he squeezed by, she looked up at him, and he gave her a harshly resentful look. Any other night, Nikolai would have remained true to his father's assessment of his nature, remaining calm and even soothing on the surface toward the woman. But tonight he was beginning to feel crazed. Even Tatyana had sensed the change in him. He felt cornered by wolves. The apartment. The school. The extra bit of money needed. And a devastating secret.

Wolves all chained together around him and barely out of reach.

Love.

He had told himself that baiting these wolves resulted from a deep love for his family. But love too had become one of the wolves because he began to question whether he was actually suffocating his family more than caring for them. When did being a good husband and father become so perilous? Did being a good man in one part of his life require wrongdoing in other parts? What could he control or change and what could he not? And even still, what should he control or change without making more of a mess? The questions had become too overwhelming to sit in his kitchen surrounded by the faint rattle of the wolves' chains.

One of the wolves was now leading the pack. There was no place to escape anymore, not even at home with his family. And when he could no longer bear those feelings, he knew he had to find a way out. One evening a few months ago, he found her online. It took him a few days to make up his mind. But once he did, he knew what he needed; it was her. Not completely, but just enough to clarify his life a bit.

Until now. He could go no further with her. Tonight he would finish it.

The snow was falling faster and stung his face in the cold gusts. Nikolai crossed the intersection to enter a plaza, glowing beneath the sky as the light reflected off of the low-hanging clouds.

Traffic sped by under the stoplight, but the cars made little sound. Somehow they softly glided across the damp pavement. Instead, laughter carried on the wind. Two young girls had begun a snowball fight on the sidewalk, and they giggled as they ran back and forth, using the legs of the adults passing by as places to hide and take cover.

One of the girls ran behind Nikolai; he stopped and looked down at her in surprise. She stared back up with her small face wrapped in a woolen hat. Nikolai examined her clear bright eyes, dimpled cheeks, and innocent smile as she looked around him from side to side, planning how to evade her antagonist.

Then she looked up at him and held a finger to her lips to entreat a secret between them, but before Nikolai could respond, he saw snow splash across her face and with an adorably playful laugh, she ran off again.

Nikolai continued through the plaza and rounded the corner onto *Neglinnaya* Street, his destination, the Ararat Park Hotel, in front of him. He climbed the sleek granite steps of the imposing building and stepped inside past the two doormen, who sized him up and then looked away.

Once through the revolving door, he entered the lobby and crossed in front of the reception desk. Waiting for the elevator, Nikolai studied the lavish lounge with its stone fireplace and Scandinavian minimalist sofas. He looked up and felt small below the never-ending vertical spiral of dark doors and space leading to a prismatic ceiling far away. It screamed affluence. He could never afford to be a guest here.

His wonder broken by the *bing* of the elevator's arrival, Nikolai stepped inside and pressed the top button. Turning around, he peered out of the glass elevator walls and watched the corridor of rooms fall below him, one after another.

Now he truly felt sick. Nikolai kept telling himself that he would end these rendezvous tonight. He would end the entire business and return his full attention to his wife and daughter. His palms were sweaty, and a hot flash passed through his body. The culmination of everything that had led to this particular moment triggered the adrenaline drilling through his nerves. For an instant, he imploded inside and closed his eyes. With another *bing,* the doors again parted. When he reopened his eyes, a dark inviting room sat ominously before him.

He knew the time would come for him to atone for his grave wrongs.

The time was now.

CHAPTER 4

Nikolai stepped forward into the bar on the top floor of the Ararat Hotel and was met by one of the immaculately dressed, striking hostesses, no doubt selectively recruited. She smiled at him. "Good evening, sir. May I help you?"

"Good evening," he replied, "I'm meeting someone who is already here."

She waved him through and followed him until he reached a few descending stairs. "Please watch your step," she advised.

"Thank you. I can find my way." With a nod, the young lady left.

As Nikolai proceeded down the steps, the city of Moscow rose before him as far as he could see. He was awestruck and, for a moment, forgot himself. The mixture of structure and luminescence seemed endless until it merely faded into the horizon.

He looked around through the sparse crowd spread out around the bar and finally saw her outline at a candlelit corner table. She had seen him first but sat motionless, simply staring back at him.

As he approached, she stayed in the deep-cushioned chair, looking out over the city.

"That's the Bolshoi down there just below us. Amazing, is it not?" she said as he arrived.

"I've never been," he replied.

"Nor have I."

Nikolai thought everything about her was elusive. Even her appearance: Raven-black hair just above the shoulder. Crimson glossed lips. The black straps of her tea-length cocktail dress invited the eyes toward the revealing v-cut neckline. It was low to the point that anyone would be tempted to imagine her shape and elegance when nude. But the martini-glass stem she held with the fingers of both hands blossoming upward reversed a meandering glance like sudden punctuation. It was as if she, herself, were also seeing every detail of her stunning mien from an outer perspective. And like some kind of dire muse, she exploited this awareness to draw a person in just close enough to unnerve them.

"I was beginning to think you wouldn't come," she said flatly.

"It's not so easy for me to get away anymore," he replied as he sat down across the small round table.

"Has your wife begun to suspect our meetings?"

"Not exactly."

She caught his implication.

"Oh really," she said with a raised eyebrow and turned to look at him squarely.

"Nataly, I love my wife. I truly love her. She's everything to me. I don't like lying to her. This has to end tonight. This is the last time."

"You control that."

"I'm ready."

They fell silent as the waitress arrived and lowered some hors d'oeuvres onto the table.

"What would you like to drink, sir?" the waitress asked.

"Nothing, thank you."

"Come now, this bar does a miraculous mint julep," Nataly prodded him.

"I'm not in the mood."

"We have time. I'm paying," she said, winking at the waitress.

"Really, no."

Nataly frowned at him playfully. "Very well then. Just the bill, please," she said to the waitress who then left. "You must play the part, Nikolai."

"I'm tired. This is too extravagant, too visible. Why here?"

"It's a good cover. It's a perfect place for the Moscow nouveau riche to meet their escorts. We are not drawing attention, and these people know how to be discreet. They don't say much if someone comes asking questions later; they're professionals. The room is on my credit card, which is not unusual when a businessman does not want to leave a paper trail of his philandering."

"Is that the reason for the dress and lipstick?" he asked.

"Exactly. Well-dressed illusion is the preferred reality these days, Nikolai. You should have learned that by now."

"Not my reality." On that point they settled at a draw and both starred out the window silently for a moment.

"And how is your wife?"

"Perplexed. My behavior is stressing her."

"She's handling your behavior gracefully. She'll be fine," Nataly said. Nikolai looked puzzled. "Your apartment is bugged. So is her office space. I've been listening. She is not 'perplexed' enough yet to discuss it with anyone. I admire her. She's remarkably stoic in nature actually. It's impressive. "

"What? How dare you!" he leaned toward her and yelled in a whisper.

"I don't take chances. It's for your safety as much as mine. You would do the same," she said. Nikolai gave her an agitated look but settled down. "What will you do after this is over?" she asked, changing the subject.

"Be a husband and a father again. Repair the damage. Going back to the things I should be doing now."

His words lingered over the table.

"You're a good man, Nikolai. A very good man. I respect that. Men like you are in short supply these days." He gave her no response. "Yes, you must continue your search for the new apartment and school. Those are important things these days," she added, raising her glass and toasting him slightly for good luck before finishing off her drink as the waitress again approached.

He gave her another agitated look. *She must have been listening to all of his discussions with Tatyana. She probably knew more about the current state of his marriage than he did.*

Nataly opened the leather cover and took out the receipt, placed cash inside, and waved "no change," as they stood up.

"Thank you. Good night," said the waitress and walked in front of them to the door.

Nataly leaned back and whispered to Nikolai, "Touch my back and smile when we pass in front of the hostesses."

He reluctantly complied, but it was an intimate, sensual touch.

CHAPTER 5

Once in the elevator, she pushed the button for the fourth floor. They stood in silence at first.

Nataly looked up at him and said with a grin, "Don't be so gloomy."

He remained silent.

She led him down the corridor to room 451, where Nataly pushed the keycard into the door and opened it. Nikolai followed her inside as she turned on the lights of a deluxe and luxuriously furnished room—as expected for this area of Moscow and this hotel in particular. A small entry hallway with the bathroom off to the right opened into the main area, featuring a meticulously made king bed, leather lounge chairs around a table, a stylish polished oak desk with a glass top, and a large flat-screen TV on top of a matching oak chest of drawers.

She stepped across the room to the floor-to-ceiling window, which looked down into a dark courtyard. Nataly pulled the curtains closed.

"How much does a room like this go for a night?" Nikolai asked.

"About $900. The cheapest type of room in the hotel," she replied, turning on a lamp and looking back over her shoulder at Nikolai.

His eyes widened. "That's about 60,000 rubles."

"Don't worry, you're worth it," she said with a laugh. From the chest of drawers, Nataly withdrew a thin laptop computer and set it on the desk.

"Let's get down to business. Let me have it," she said.

Nikolai reached into his pocket and brought out a small blue USB memory stick. "That's all of it," he said.

She took the storage drive and motioned for him to sit on the edge of the bed. She opened the laptop; the screen cast a pale glow as it came to life. Then she plugged the memory stick into the computer and tapped the touch pad to open its contents.

Nataly looked up at Nikolai in disbelief.

"It's the best I could do," he replied. "It's all there. Believe me."

There were hundreds of folders on the first screen, each marked with a number, such as 4.13, 7.02, and 12.28. She clicked one of them. And then clicked again to open a file.

"But this," she motioned at the screen, "this does not make any sense."

She turned the screen to Nikolai. It showed a Wikipedia entry in Russian for Casamba, a genus of moth. She clicked on another file. It was in Hindi with a photo of a telescope.

"Nikolai, what's going on here? What are all these Wikipedia files?"

He sighed. "In fact, it's every Wikipedia entry in every one of its 278 languages for the last year."

"Two hundred and seventy-eight! The last year?" she replied.

"Yes, each folder represents one day and contains 278 files, which are a complete copy of Wikipedia for that day in each language. Not only that, but the articles are not in alphabetical order, they are in a random order."

She rubbed her fingers across her eyes and looked back at him for some explanation.

"That's the encryption," Nikolai added.

"Wikipedia pages are the encryption?"

"Think about it. It's perfect for hiding information. Wikipedia is organic. Each day it evolves: Additional pages are added. Existing pages are altered and some are subtracted. Words change within the articles. And then the whole thing is randomized. There's no pattern. The code is unbreakable without a key. It might not even have one single key—perhaps there are hundreds or thousands—mostly because you don't know where the encryption begins or ends. It's there, but where?"

"Exactly," she exclaimed, "what am I supposed to do with this? You promised to bring me the specific information we needed. Wouldn't you agree that some form of superencrypted system is a bit short of that?"

"I told you I would get you what I could. The base files here, and I have half of the cypher. At least the first one."

"Half?"

"The cypher has two parts: first, you need to know the day, and then you need to know the pattern of words, numbers, or whatever within that day."

He stopped. She said nothing.

"I think I know the day," he continued, "and you will have to locate the other half."

"Where?"

"I don't know exactly."

"What do you mean you don't know? How am *I* supposed to find it then?"

"You are an investigative journalist. Do the things a person like you normally does."

"How am I supposed to do that? I can't exactly ask around for something like this. You came to me, Nikolai, saying you had the information. Now this? We're both in too deep to leave it unfinished."

"Look, here is what I do know from a guy working in our department, Artyom Chuchin. He had been educated in math and was very clever. Not a genius, but very good. He was awkward with people in the office generally and a bit paranoid, so we mostly left him on his own. The company employs cryptographers at various levels to encode sensitive records—for example: invoices, purchase orders, confidential contracts, and the correspondence trails approving transactions and requisitions. He did this for the accounting department. After I had created and collected the original records, I passed them off to Artyom for encryption. That was not unusual."

"So?"

"He disappeared shortly after he encoded the documents we need."

"Disappeared?"

"Vanished. When he didn't turn up for work after a few days, people became curious. Someone went to his apartment, and we only heard he had left a note for his landlady saying he wanted more from life. He was going to travel the world. He apologized for not returning the key or ending the lease formally. He told her to do whatever she liked with all his belongings."

"So you expect me to track down this Artyom in the mountains of Nepal or on a tropical island?" she asked coolly.

"He wasn't the type to suddenly leave, especially on some world journey."

"What do you mean 'he wasn't the type'? How do you know? It sounds like a reasonable story to me. He probably was burned out from looking at numbers all day."

"He wasn't the type of person to do that," Nikolai said firmly. "Listen to me. I know the people in my profession. I see their psychological profiles before they are assigned to my department; it's a sensitive department. Artyom was odd, but he was stable."

Nataly sat back in her chair. "Suppose you're right. Supposed he didn't just disappear but was kidnapped or assassinated instead. Must that be connected to *these* particular files? As you say, he dealt with many sensitive documents—any one of them might have been the reason."

"I kept my eye on this data because something was unusual about the account from the start. I checked the records every day on the internal data server to see if he had encrypted them yet. The day he stopped coming to work was the day after the files had apparently been encrypted, and I no longer had access to them. That also is not unusual. However, two days after he disappeared the whole account had ceased to exist. No trace. As far as I could tell, the same had not happened to any other recent files he had processed. And this is why I began to dig around a bit, carefully."

"You told me from the beginning that you already knew everything," she said.

"I generally know what the payments were for, which is why I contacted you. I knew we had transferred the necessary funds; the cash flow progressed from our subsidiary accounts elsewhere. The *real* questions are: who made the original payment order, and where did the money go? That information was scattered, as I told you from the beginning. Now I know, and now *you* know, these Wikipedia files are the missing link... somehow. I've done my part."

She shook her head. "But if you could get all of that, why not just get the original? Why only this encrypted version?"

"There's no original version anymore. What you have is the only remaining evidence. Do you understand me? Except for these files, there's *no* proof that anything ever happened. If this USB storage is erased or destroyed, no one will ever know. And the only reason we have these files now is because they were tucked away on a backup server. It was only an afterthought to check. Only by chance."

"Chance?"

"Whoever wanted the account records to disappear knew what they were doing. It was deliberate. They not only erased the originals, but they also sanitized the versions stored on the backup servers. All of our records are backed up nightly. The last thirty days are stored completely."

Nikolai paused. Then he continued.

"Yet, the original encrypted files—the versions encrypted in the normal method—were erased from all of the backup servers as well. Plus, the Wikipedia files began discreetly appearing on the same backups from the first day I handed Arytom the account files for encryption. The Wikipedia files must contain a second copy, a duplication, embedded but complete."

Nikolai hesitated.

"But...," he hesitated again, "all of these Wikipedia files also went missing after I accessed them and copied them to this USB memory stick. Someone must have looked at them after I did and was worried enough to remove them, because they probably had no idea why these odd Wikipedia pages were on the servers at all. In fact, after that, everything Arytom had worked on for the last month had been deleted. This has to be the proof. Now you have the only evidence that still exists. If Artyom thought ahead enough to hide a copy of the documents on our server, he certainly also hid a copy of the cypher somewhere. You can find it."

"But you really don't know, do you?" she said forcefully. "You're guessing, making massive fanciful claims about what these files mean. Claims with unimaginable consequences. Unthinkable! To prove your delusion, you bring me gibberish Wikipedia entries with scarce possibility of discovering what they really mean."

"No, no," he replied, "I know everything is hidden here. About a week before he vanished, Artyom asked me to lunch. He wanted to discuss his future with *Petrovaryagi*. He had never wanted to speak with me outside the office before, so I thought he probably wanted to ask for a promotion. He didn't though. We mostly made small talk. Two things seemed especially odd in the conversation. At one awkward moment, he described an unbreakable system of concealing information. He didn't say Wikipedia specifically. He called it 'steganography,' hiding things in plain sight. This fits with what he described."

Nikolai gave Nataly a look as if to nudge her belief with his eyes.

"What about the second thing?" she asked.

"While we were walking back to the office he mentioned the day he started working for the company: 10 December."

"Why is that odd?"

"I thought about it after he disappeared and realized that was *not* the day he started at *Petrovaryagi*. Even though it was a few years ago, I remember his first day because he walked into my office an hour late, dripping water on my floor. His clothes were soaked with rain. I sent him home and told him to try again the next day. It was in the summer, not winter. I checked. His employee file began on 10 June."

Nataly shook her head in disbelief.

"Nikolai, you are a madman. Youre wasting my time and putting us in a lot of danger."

Nikolai jumped to his feet. "It's true. It happened! And the proof is in these files, damn it!" Then he caught himself. "I've risked everything to bring you this: my job, my marriage, everything I hold dear. It's not in my best interest to be in contact with you. Why would I do so if I didn't believe it..." He stopped and took a deep breath.

"Believe what? Tell me one more time. Make me believe too."

"Don't. Please don't make me. I can't describe it again. It's too horrible," he said calmly.

"Okay, you don't have to." Her tone changed. "My instincts trust you completely now. Only the truth can be unspeakable, because sometimes it is inconceivable otherwise. If these files hold what you say, then it's more than just a crime. The world will know because of you. This is the type of crime history does not forget nor forgive. The consequences are unimaginable."

"Yes. I often overlook and erase minor misconducts for *Petrovaryagi*. The little things. The costs of doing business in a competitive market. A bribe here and there. Okay, fine. Move on. But this is unconscionable. Why do something like this? To all those people? The complicity from top to bottom. Even me...especially me. But this once, I can say 'enough.' Maybe that counts for something."

The words lingered between them.

She continued, "Nikolai, I believe you. I believe all of this is as staggering as you say it is. I know you are not a madman. You stand by your convictions when it would be better and much easier for you to look the other way. You really have risked everything, especially with your finances already tight. That is proof enough for me."

She looked up at him with caring, passionate eyes.

For the first time in months Nikolai felt as though another human being had heard the deafening cries of all those people that echoed in him day and night since he had learned the truth. He sensed that she was a woman who understood her own wolves too.

"I've done everything I can do to make this right. It's off my shoulders, and I'm finished," he said.

She nodded at first and then abruptly stopped. "Wait," she said, "go back. Did you say the Wikipedia files were deleted immediately *after* you accessed them?"

"Yes."

"Then you realize someone knows you found them. Nikolai you've been compromised."

"I considered the possibility beforehand. Every computer in the company is monitored. That's routine. I opened a hundred or so files and moved them around the same day I copied these and others in bulk. I even searched different days of the backup to make it look like I had just lost something and was trying to recover it. The existence of the strange files was noticed but not my particular interest in them. The whole month was deleted. Everything is encrypted, remember. I'm thought to be very loyal. And I've been utterly loyal, until now. I wouldn't be suspected. And I've been careful since then. Nothing out of the ordinary has happened. I'm fine. And you said yourself that you've been listening and watching."

"No one followed you into the bar tonight. I guess you're right," she agreed.

She stood up and walked over to the small refrigerator in the room and turned around, holding a bottle of ice-cold Stolichnaya Elit. Then, out of the chest of drawers under the mirror she produced a bottle of Talisker whisky. She stood in front of Nikolai with one in each hand.

"I believe this calls for a drink. Even though it is a grim moment, let us commemorate the end of our time together and, more importantly, a courageous man," she said with a playful smile upon her lips. "Will you be having whisky or vodka, sir?"

Nikolai smiled. He really smiled for the first time in a long time. "I've a deep fondness for Scottish water," he replied.

"I thought you might say that. I'll stay closer to Mother Russia tonight and continue with vodka myself. East and West together," she laughed.

Nataly walked over to the glasses, opened the bottles, and began to pour. As she did, she pushed her hair back to reveal her neck and loosened a button on the front of her blouse.

"Promise me you'll find the key. Break the code." Nikolai pleaded with earnestness.

She turned around with the glasses in hand. "I guarantee you I'll find the other half of the key next," she said seriously and with a tinge of ominousness. Then she tilted her face a bit and teasingly added, "Nikolai, I always find what I search for. I get what I want. And I always seek out handsome, courageous men."

The words lingered echoing in the silence.

She laughed. Nikolai laughed a little too, looked away, and returned to find her staring at him intensely, powerfully.

"No doubt you do get what you want," he said almost inaudibly.

Nataly walked toward him, almost curling against his frame. She looked up and admired the contours of his face as she placed the glass of whisky in his hand.

She backed up just enough to see into his eyes. "*Na Zdorovie*, Nikolai," she said and took a sip.

"*Na Zdorovie*," he replied somewhat awkwardly.

As Nikolai raised his glass, she stepped in closer again and lightly pressed her breasts against him. She put her hand upon the side of his face. He stopped and looked down at her. She exuded seduction, total pleasure, and total eroticism.

"These past few months must have been so difficult for you, Nikolai. You must be emotionally exhausted. Look at how tense you are. What you have done is a great thing. You deserve a small pleasure."

She kissed him on cheek and whispered, "Put the glass down. I'll give you that gift of pleasure. I want you to take me now. Let me say goodbye in my own way. The best way."

Her hand moved down his body, as she kissed his neck and then moved up for his lips. But he stood there unmoved. She was not to have his lips. He peeled away and leaned back against the desk.

"You're very kind, Nataly, and beautiful. I love my wife. Only Tatyana."

He offered no words of apology or soothing regret. He took a long sip of the whisky. It warmed his mouth wonderfully.

She nodded. "You're a good man. A very good man."

And she looked at him with great pity.

It was the third time he had heard those words this evening, and they were the last thing Nikolai remembered before the lightheadedness. The room began to spin. He dropped the glass and tried to lean against the wall, but instead collapsed on the floor.

Nataly sat down in the chair and watched him lying unconscious at her feet. A minute later, two men quietly entered the room. She looked up at them and said, "Get him on the bed quickly. Strip him naked. The sedative wears off fast."

CHAPTER 6

Nikolai opened his eyes.

He did not know where he was—or, for a few seconds, who he was. But he felt blissful and translucent.

He realized he was in a bed. His eyes began to clear. On top of him was a woman with a gorgeous body.

He could not have known that he had been drugged with a potent mix of distilled THC, Bremelanotide, MDMA, Vardenafil, and a sharp short-term tranquilizer to make him manageable in the beginning. It had worked. He was beyond high and incredibly aroused.

Each moment seemed continuous, one tied perfectly to the next. He experienced it in flashes, sometimes obscurely and other times with superhuman lucidity and sensitivity. There was no paradox, only the connectedness of all space and time.

His sight fully returned first. The dark room brightened as ambient light poured in around the curtains, creating a tangled mixture of palely illuminated skin and shadows. Nikolai looked down to see part of himself reappearing and glistening as she drew upward, only to be taken in again when she descended with force. This woman rotated her hips, straightened her lower back, and then continued to rise and fall with rhythm and speed.

When did this start?

Her torso was taut and sloping backward. Her breasts recorded the collisions. Now sound returned. Except for her deep breaths, blending with the rustle of sheets against the mattress and following each impression into the bed, the noiselessness was deafening.

The woman's face and gaze lowered from the ceiling. Their eyes locked. Her stare was hateful and violent in the seconds before she smiled vaguely. She left him again when her eyes closed, and her mouth fell open during the short rapid jolts back and forth. She alternated pace and depth.

Who is this woman? I know her, but who?

Nikolai was large, and the repetitive exertions of her inner thighs showed the considerable effort she had to make to have all of him. Each time she came back down, he felt himself fill her; his confused apprehension finally dissolved into erotic pleasure.

Nikolai relaxed as instinct took over. He reached up and cupped her breasts, rolling her sex-hardened nipples beneath his thumbs. The hallucinations from the MDMA set in. His soul was bursting with emotional tenderness, and he felt himself pouring his soul into her with each touch. Nikolai could no longer comprehend loneliness; he and the woman had become the same—a unified reality. He had never felt such flawless euphoria. He desperately wanted to share everything with her, and he sensed she desperately wanted to understand him.

The woman bent forward, placing a hand on the pillow slightly above Nikolai's head to steady herself. She descended near his chest slowly with deeper swivel movements. Nikolai could feel her ass doing the work. Again she watched his eyes, sizing up his thoughts and emotions. Then she finally kissed him. Her head raised and her chest lowered deeper. He felt her breasts sway across him, each beautiful cell of her body intimately stroking him with care. The sensation of her flushed skin on one side of him contrasted with the crisp fresh coolness of the cotton sheet enveloping his silhouette on the other side.

"You feel so good inside me. Do you like it?" she asked.

He did not reply.

She kissed him again. "Nothing exists. Let go and enjoy this," the woman whispered.

He felt his hands on her back and wondered how they got there.

"Do you like fucking me?" she asked again.

"Yes," he said as he found his voice.

She had him completely now. There was no resistance, no inhibition.

"Good. Do you feel that? You fill me completely. I am slayed, Nikolai. Slayed straight through. Amazing. Now take me from behind."

She kissed him again, pulled off, and rolled over. When he sat up, the hallucinations started.

For Nikolai it was fascinating to step outside himself and watch as she untethered from him and drifted off into space. Just before the point where she would have disappeared, he saw her rise up on her hands and knees. The back of her legs and her ass radiated vividly in the soft light, while the rest of her body plunged into the darkness of everything around them.

He reentered his body and followed her. It was pure and it was carnal. His senses were overwhelmed—smell, touch, sight, sound—all of it brought a flow within him, one wave after the next of epiphany.

One hand was on her waist, and the other held himself as his tip penetrated her. She tensed and her shoulders expanded. With both hands wrapped firmly around her waist, he flexed and pushed in halfway. She exhaled and sighed. He stopped. Nikolai examined her, not out of caution, but with a curiosity of fondness and a liberated sadism.

"Sink it all in," she told him as she looked back to the side.

He gripped her and did as she said. One smooth solid thrust. She was silent but her body was focused. When she felt his thighs against her finally, she pushed her hair back with one hand. Then she lowered her face down to the mattress. Taking another breath, she drove herself backward and up onto him, making sure that she got that little extra too.

The curvy, soft figure wrapped around him was a composite satisfaction of all his subconscious desires, those he was unaware of until now. She was all the things he had denied himself. He felt her as he had never felt a woman before. She completely melded to him without a past or future. An enlightenment glowed brighter within both of them.

He drew back slowly and savored the sensation of the cool night, following him out of her, and the soaking heat, bidding him back inside. Nikolai tilted a little and entered her again, working through her resistance. The snugness passed along all sides him.

Back and forth in the oneness. Nikolai was at the peak of his high now.

He could see through her skin, muscle tissue, bones, and organs straight to her very center. She was pure fusion. He watched himself sliding into her again and again with a steady finesse. Each time, the colors in her core grew brighter with pleasure. Suddenly, the moment was shattered when the woman pierced the wondrous incandescence with her voice: "Fuck. Me. Hard."

That voice rattled in mind. It was furious love. His ass muscles tightened. He put one hand on her lower back, holding her down.

And he fucked her hard.

The muffled sound of their sex echoed from the walls. A chorus of haunting drums formed in his mind, a divine voodoo percussion. In the distance he faintly heard her moans, but he was far away again. A bright glow enveloped his body, but he looked down at her in the inky darkness.

Her face pitched up again, and he saw its outline in the mirror. She lunged forward with each absorbed impact. Time stretched out seamlessly in all directions around them. Nikolai had never had something so rough also be so tranquil. What he gave her was beyond any capacity he had felt before.

Never had he contained such a robust energy. Never had he been so savage and so tender in the same instant. A momentum beyond his comprehension. Vitality rushed through his veins from some unknown source.

Where?

And then he felt it. Full. Never like this. A sensation known and unknown. A perfect pulse, starting at the top of his ass and moving under his waist at limitless speed, but suspended forever. It shot down his shaft. He watched it within him gaining force as it went. He drilled deep into her once more.

Do not leave me behind yet.

At once there was a great wailing cry in a wilderness. Nikolai's body was surrounded by a white forest. Then instantly elsewhere, a crooked highway through a frozen desert of taiga stretched before him. The mountains in the distance were made low and the valleys raised. The rough asphalt became smooth and fine. An invisible force suddenly pulled the road straight until it fell over the horizon. And the glory of the brilliant first spark in all things was revealed.

Nikolai orgasmed.

All faded and he was back in the room again. Everything in his body collapsed and sank after he came, and he fell to the bed. He watched her shudder repugnantly with satisfaction as she felt his release. Suddenly, a new emotion flooded him: terror.

But she followed him backward on the bed. She held a cup to his lips. He drank from it. Another bitter cocktail. She kept it against his lips. He drank more. Another swallow.

Once again, Nikolai went unconscious.

CHAPTER 7

Cold water thrown across his face brought Nikolai back to consciousness. He felt the sharp headache.

A large hand slapped him. "Wake up," a gruff voice ordered.

Nikolai opened his eyes with painful sobriety. A bear of a man with dark, cool eyes stared down at him. The first feature Nikolai noticed was his mostly bald head with tightly cropped hair around the ears. Given his thick, round face and tree trunk for a neck, the man had the appearance of an Olympic weightlifter. Nikolai noticed a prison tattoo on his neck—a skull with a knife through it and dripping blood. The skull and knife were surrounded by barbed wire laced with the outline of a rose and stem. Underneath it were the letters "ЯТУ".

The bear turned his head. Looking off to the side, he said, "He's back."

The man slapped Nikolai once more for good measure and then stepped away, his shadow now gone. Nikolai's body lay exhausted and limp on the bed.

What happened?

Fragments of memory found their way to the surface. He held his hand up to block the light and squinted to look around. Nataly leaned forward in a chair. The side of her face was lit by the austere lamp, but only enough for her visage to gradually vanish back into the darkness like the moon in phase. She gave no expression for Nikolai to read. Even the glint of the vodka in her hands stood motionless.

"What is this? What have you done to me?" Nikolai said as he shook his head, regaining clarity.

"Be calm, Nikolai. There's no need to get excited."

He looked around. Now Nikolai could clearly see that the bear was, indeed, as big as a doorway and nicely dressed in dark trousers and a button-up shirt under a leather jacket. To say he looked serious and formidable was an understatement.

To his right sat another comparatively younger man in jeans and a gray sweater. He had a broad, round face except for his square jaw. A little shorter than Nikolai, although stockier, the man looked somewhat Central Asian: dark eyes, black straight hair, wide eyebrows, and a slightly darker tone to his skin—a mixture of Slavic and Chinese features.

His scowl and aggressive stance were awkwardly thuggish, like a shy, timid man trying to act the part.

"Who are these guys, Nataly? What are they doing here? What is going on?"

She calmly took out a cigarette and lit it methodically. "I'm changing the nature of our relationship," she said smoothly.

"What do you mean 'change'? What is there to change? We're supposed to help each other!"

"Don't shout, Nikolai. I can hear you just fine. Settle down. Yes, you've helped me, and, yes, I'm going to help you. This is a very complicated matter you have gotten yourself into. More complicated than you know. I'm not the compassionate investigative journalist you think I am, and I have no intention of making the information you gave me public. Let's just say I'm here to fix things for everyone involved. That includes you now. But I need you to be rational."

"I'm naked on a bed. There are two strangers with us, and I have no idea what you are talking about. Explain what the hell is going on right now."

She took a slow drag on the cigarette and then exhaled. It reminded him of how Tatyana had looked when he left their apartment.

He glanced at the clock next to the bed. Only two and a half hours had passed, but to Nikolai, it seemed closer to morning.

She was in control and slowing things down, and he realized it.

"Nikolai," she said tonelessly, "when I usually have this kind of conversation with a someone, it follows a progression: I first leverage their friends, then their finances, and finally their families. The idea is to start with the least amount of damage and build up to the next level, hoping they will break early for their own sake. And they always break. It's just a matter of what they lose before they do. But you have stolen valuable information from serious people, and the damage it could do to them is so absolute that I have to make an exception for you and go in reverse order."

She paused for her words to sink in. Nikolai had regained his bearings but still breathed uneasily.

Nataly continued, "First, family. You and I just had sex if you do not remember. The entire room was wired. There are photos, an audio recording, and video."

She nodded at the big guy. He placed an iPad showing a series of photos on the bed next to Nikolai.

"Look at the photos," she told him.

At this point, Nikolai was aware he was being handled. The thought of what was on the tablet sent cold steel down his spine. He made no movement and returned Nataly's stare.

"Look at the photos, Nikolai." Still he sat in motionless resistance. "Look at the goddamn photos, or this is going to get ugly quickly," she said slowly without raising her voice.

Nikolai moved his hand across the bed covers and picked up the tablet. He peered down at the first image and moved through the others with a slide of his finger. They were from multiple angles. All were clear and graphic. At the end of the series was indeed a video. He played it for a few seconds and then clicked it off. Some kind of sensitive low-light lens had been used because every detail of his face was clear, as well as his words responding to her whispers. He had obviously enjoyed it.

Yet, Nataly's face was obscured or never in the light. On some only her chin and mouth were visible. Others showed a strange side angle, beginning closely from her ear down to her neck with the focus more on Nikolai in the background, just enough to capture his orgasm and pleasure.

Still, one shot had her eyes: a photo of her on her knees with Nikolai behind, and she was looking directly at the camera. Her expression evidenced a moment in which she was receiving something, not with reluctance, but with vigor and desire.

No photo allowed piecing together her identity. This was the design, he realized, but cleverly done so that it would not appear intentional.

Her silence while he looked at the photos and the video sealed the effect.

Nikolai glanced back up at Nataly with a look of disgust. "That's not me. I'm not that man. You know that."

"Yes, but does your wife know that? Nikolai, I know how much you love her. And I know how much she loves you. I know these facts like I know everything else about you. I've studied you, and I've studied her. She really does love you, and she has never cheated on you. Not once. But you…now…"

Nataly paused for a moment and then continued.

"Now, you can guess how this works. What you are getting is a one-time offer. If you refuse, I guarantee the following events: Tomorrow morning Tatyana will wake up to this iPad leaning against your apartment door and also the number of this hotel room, where you will still be drunkenly passed out. She will believe these photos were provided by a wealthy jealous husband who had hired an investigator. She will find you here, and no doubt you will try to explain. Who knows what you will say? That it's not what it seems? That you were forced to? You're the victim of some plot?

"Despite what she says about modern marriage, she will be crushed by the lies you so resolutely and definitively told her before you left your apartment. Although disoriented and devastated, your marriage could probably recover from just the photos. But the audio and video? Which do you think will be more painful, her listening to the sounds of you fucking me or the video images replaying in her head of our bodies for years and years? She will wonder why these things are being sent to her, but deep down she will accept it's simply revenge for you sleeping with another man's wife. Lies upon lies. Remember, tonight she told you that she cannot handle secrets. Not like her vulnerable mother had to endure from her father."

Nikolai gave no sign of his feelings. He matched Nataly's composure second for second.

"Finances," she continued. "Just when Tatyana is beginning to process your infidelity, a week or so later, she will suddenly learn that her company is downsizing and she will lose her job. She will plunge into fear and dismay about not being able to afford a new apartment and the new school for little Anastasia. But she will find no comfort in your savings account."

At this point, Nataly tried to gauge how close he was to breaking, but again his face was blank, his breathing calm.

"I know about the two bank accounts: your joint checking account with Tatyana for living costs but also the savings account with which she trusts you completely. If you decline my offer, your savings account will be immediately drained. After she loses her job, she will see hotel bills, gambling receipts, and credit card charges for luxury female gifts emptying your savings account. What I tell you is true. Don't doubt me. I will, of course, leave a little money in the checking account. I don't want your family to starve, at least not quickly. But does a small amount of money hurt more than it helps by constantly reminding her that your family barely has enough to get by? Too little is often worse than none at all. With each bill she opens, she will ache from the financial stress."

Nataly stubbed out the cigarette.

"Imagine where Tatyana will be emotionally by this point—her marriage wrecked, her job gone, and her savings philandered away. If she is still holding herself together, I will decide what button to push next. You see, Nikolai, the goal is to send her into a nervous breakdown. That's what I get paid to do, to make an example out of you so that others will not follow the same path."

Nataly paused.

"But it's not really about you, your marriage, her sanity, or even your finances. These are only a means to a greater end. The person I really want to damage is Anastasia. The best way to do that is to ensure that she grows up in a broken home, recalling a worthless father who drove her mother to insanity and poverty. You know, Nikolai, they say these early years determine the rest of a child's life. You can spend decades trying to repair the damage I inflict, but over the next few months, Anastasia will be irreparably twisted. How do you think she will turn out after such a deformed start? In a poor school? Making friends? Eventually getting a job? Discovering men? Happiness? Her own family? How do you imagine this all ends? There is nothing you can do to protect little Stasya from me."

That cold feeling in his spine now shivered throughout Nikolai's entire body.

"Oh, and friends. That one is simple really. You have very few besides Tatyana and your daughter.

Most of them are colleagues. How long will you be able to stay functioning at work or carry on a meaningful conversation with anyone with all of this happening? *Petrovaryagi* is not going to fire you. On the contrary, the company with trap you by making sure no one else in Russia will hire you, and then they will squeeze your career until you are miserable in the office, each day doing menial paperwork. But there will be nowhere else for you to go. You will be completely isolated and alienated. Disdained and pitied, like a leper. Do you know what suffering really is? Suffering is slow. Suffering is gradual. Suffering is knowing exactly what is happening and being powerless to stop it."

She leaned closer.

"But here is the catch. None of this has happened— yet. And none of it ever needs to. You will never see me again. You will not profit by any of this, but you would wake up tomorrow as well off as you are today and with a positive reference from *Petrovaryagi* to another company somewhere else. And that is a blessing. You and your family can continue in life as you were, *if* you agree to my offer."

She let those words settle.

"If you do not, I work for extremely unsympathetic and severe people, and I will have no choice but to take you, your family—your daughter—beyond a point that anyone should have to suffer. And you, Nikolai, you control this moment completely."

"So what is this offer?" he asked.

Nataly looked at the bear and then the other guy. Then back at Nikolai. The bear took a piece of paper and pen out of his coat pocket and placed them on the bed next to Nikolai.

"That you forget about this." She held up the USB memory stick. "Sign the nondisclosure agreement, and never discuss what you know with anyone. If you ever speak of it after signing this agreement, you will lose everything. You have no evidence, so it would only annoy very well-connected and powerful individuals, who would immediately have you committed to a mental institution. Wipe it from your mind, Nikolai. That's all. Very simple. Go home."

Nikolai sighed deeply at those words. Hearing that deal, he knew the answer and closed his eyes.

"You…" he said as he opened them again, "are a sick bitch. Who are you? Who are you, really? Do you take pleasure in doing this?"

The bear stepped up and raised his hand to slap the aggression out of Nikolai, but Nataly waved him off.

"Yes," she said, "I do. I do take pleasure in this. And that is exactly what I am. A sick bitch who will take

Anastasia to hell with me. I will be merciless with your daughter. I will enjoy it. But I hope you accept my offer. The choice is yours."

Nikolai picked up the iPad.

"And these pictures? Sex? There were other ways. Or do you always take this kind of pleasure from the people you hurt before you crush them, body and soul?"

"No. You're just a job. I didn't even feel the sex. It was the most effective way of cutting into you. Your flaw is that you really are a good man who loves his wife faithfully. If only you had basic ordinary corruptions like other men, it would have been unnecessary. Such a pity."

She could have gone further with her reply to slice him deeper, but it would have been a waste. She knew him well enough to know that she had bled him to the limit. Any more and he might go numb and give up the bit of hope necessary to push him in the right direction, the way out. The only remaining question was whether his love for his family outweighed what he knew about something that had happened far away to people with whom he had no connection. He could not bring those people back from the dead, but surely he would realize his family could live normally, happily. She desperately hoped so.

"Nikolai, I'm here to help you. You believe that, don't you? That I'm here to help you?"

The words went right past him.

"This is a one-time offer. Now," she said, making sure he could see her seriousness.

He was silent for a moment, filled with emotion and whirling thoughts, although cool and steady on the surface. But she knew the truth. She knew this moment well. Every time she had done this, the people always reacted the same. He was torn, like the others, as deeply torn as any human can be. He would make the right decision and walk away. She opened her mouth to give him another push. Just one more small push and he would go home.

And then she saw something she had never seen before.

At the exact moment he should have broken, he cut her off before she could speak.

Without any trembling or hesitation in his voice, Nikolai spoke. "No. I love them more than anything else in life. I believe you will do what you say. I believe every word. And we will still rebuild as a family as best we can. Listen and listen well, if the only choice is between my family and the horror hidden within those documents, then I must choose *not* to forget."

Nataly did not hesitate one moment either. There was nothing more to be said.

She held out her hand.

The smaller guy stepped forward and handed her a black Glock 28.

From the corner of his eye, Nikolai saw the gun, and he instinctively ran naked for the door. He almost got to it before the bear reached around his neck, choking him and compressing his vocal chords while pulling him back. He held Nikolai up for a second and crushed his trachea, which made a distinctive crunching sound, before tossing him down on the floor with shattering force.

Nikolai was dazed and gasping as he pushed himself up against the wall.

Nataly stepped over and knelt down with him. Nikolai saw the gun again and the survival instinct brought him back into focus. He started to reach up.

She put her hand across his mouth as he wheezed, "Please, no," and pushed the gun firmly against his chest. The muffled blast of the .380 bullet made less noise than someone punching the wall. His hands dropped. His body convulsed as the bullet penetrated his right ventricle; encountering his rapid heartbeat, the cardiovascular muscle tore apart followed by the piercing of his lower esophagus.

Blood ran between the fingers of her hand covering his mouth. She watched his eyes intently as he went into shock when his blood pressure dropped.

Nikolai heaved a soaked, bloody breath and blacked out into death.

Nataly looked at the two men as she stood up. They were putting on gloves. "Mess the room up. Take his wallet and watch so they will think it was a robbery or drug dealers intending it to look like a robbery. Wipe the fingerprints from the room. Here's the gun. Do your thing. Let's go."

She stepped into the bathroom and raised the handle on the faucet with the back of her hand. Nikolai's blood washed into the basin, the water becoming ever clearer until the last of it was gone.

In the mirror she saw herself. Her own eyes were slightly more dead, empty and looking back at her in the same way she had looked at Nikolai. The sight of herself made her forget to breathe. Then she snapped out of it, turned the water off, and stepped back into the hallway. The two guys were efficient and fast as usual. Everything was ready.

The smaller one went to the door and looked through the peephole.

"It's clear," he said as he opened the door and slid out.

The bear stopped near Nataly and without looking at her said, "You knew he wouldn't take the deal, didn't you?"

"Yes. Knowing what he knew, would you?"

The bear shrugged in deference.

"Then why didn't you just shoot him when he was still drugged instead of fucking him and going through everything else. It would have looked better if he was in the bed. You're losing your touch."

"Suffering. This is my last one. I wanted to watch him suffer. One for the road, you know."

"He was right. You are a sick, ruthless bitch," the bear said. With a smile on his lips, he motioned for her to leave first.

She went straight out with a bold nonchalance instead of checking down the corridor. The bear turned off the lights and closed the door silently. He did take the time to look down the corridor. No one.

The amber digits of the clock next to the bed across the room from Nikolai's lifeless body read 02:43.

ABOUT THE AUTHOR

A native son of Mississippi, Mitch holds a Ph.D. in International Law and a full-time day job. 22:10 is the result of very early-mornings and an overactive imagination.

He lives in Arlington, Virginia, after more than a decade in Wales, Beijing, Geneva, Oslo, and Edinburgh. No aspect whatsoever of 22:10 is autobiographical other than geography.

Mitch is 36 and works in the area of human rights law.

AUTHOR'S NOTE

For background and notes on 22:10, as well as notifications on the release of forthcoming installments, visit

www.huckleberryink.com

If you enjoyed 22:10, the best way to support the story is to give each individual part a positive review on the Amazon website. Incidentally, Amazon does not accept your 'stars' review unless you also include some text.

Thanks to Jill Welsh for her remarkable editing.